Debutante Hill

Lois Duncan

LIZZIE
SKURNICK
BOOKS

Brooklyn, New York

Printed in the United States
Reissue Edition
10 9 8 7 6 5 4 3 2 1

Please direct inquiries to:
Lizzie Skurnick Books
an imprint of Ig Publishing
392 Clinton Avenue #1S
Brooklyn, NY 11238
www.igpub.com

Library of Congress Cataloging-in-Publication Data

Duncan, Lois, 1934-
  Debutante Hill / Lois Duncan.
     pages cm
  Originally published in New York by Dodd, Mead, 1958.
  Summary: In the 1950s, when the society families of Rivertown
decide to launch their daughters in an elaborate debut season, beau-
tiful Lynn Chambers is delighted until her father refuses to let her
participate in this display of snobbishness and Lynn finds herself
ostracized from the community in which she grew up.
  ISBN 978-1-939601-00-1
  [1. Debutantes--Fiction. 2. Social classes--Fiction. 3. Belonging
(Social psychology)--Fiction. 4. Dating (Social customs)--Fiction.
5. Love--Fiction.] I. Title.
  PZ7.D9117De 2013
  [Fic]--dc23
                                          2013022631

To Mother

INTRODUCTION

I can't remember a time when I didn't think of myself as a writer. I started submitting stories to magazines when I was ten, painstakingly pecking them out on my mother's manual typewriter, and shipping them off to the addresses of publications I found on my parents' coffee table.

Needless to say, those manuscripts were quickly returned.

The editor of *Ladies Home Journal* was kinder than the others. Instead of a form rejection slip, she sent me a personal note that said, "Try us again in ten years." That bewildered me, as I had not disclosed my age and thought no one would guess I was a child.

Rather than stopping me, those rejections stirred me on to greater activity. My writing attempts became more and more ambitious. Tales of flaming romance, blood spurting violence, pain and passion, lust and adventure, flew back and forth to New York in a steady stream. My parents thought me cute and funny. My teachers thought me horrid and precocious. As for myself, I was proud. While my schoolmates were playing jacks and trading comic books, I—plump, bespectacled, and unimpressive as I might appear—was plunging ahead toward the glorious career that I was certain would be my destiny.

Three years passed, and I accumulated so many rejection slips that my mother made me stop saving them.

"After all, dear, once you've read one of them, you've read them all."

Then one day I came home from school to find a craggy-faced giant of a man occupying the living room sofa. He was a new neighbor who had just moved in down the beach from our home in Sarasota, Florida, and he was a writer. His name was MacKinlay Kantor.

"Lois," my father said after introductions had been made, "why don't you show Mr. Kantor that story of yours that came back yesterday from the *Saturday Evening Post*?" He did not have to ask me twice. What an opportunity! A published author was right there waiting to appreciate me! I rushed to get the story and stood expectantly at his elbow as Mr. Kantor scanned the pages.

The praise I anticipated did not come.

"My dear," Mr. Kantor exploded, "this is pure shit!"

It was the first time that word had ever been used in my hearing. My mother was as shocked as I was.

"Mack," she said reprovingly, "Lois is only thirteen!"

"I don't care how old she is," my idol roared. "If she is putting her stories into the market and expects somebody to buy them, she is old enough to take criticism. What kind of subject matter is this for a kid? She's never had a love affair or seen a man get murdered. Good writing comes from the heart, not off the top of the head."

He turned to me and added more gently, "Throw this stuff in the trash, child, and go write a story about something you know about. Write something that rings true."

I was crushed. I was also challenged. Later that week I

did write a story about a fat, shy little girl with braces and glasses who covered her insecurity by writing stories about imaginary adventures. I submitted it to a teen publication, and by return mail I received a check for twenty-five dollars.

That was one of the most incredible moments of my life.

From then on, my fate was decided. I wrote what I knew about, and could hardly wait to rush home from school each day to fling myself at the typewriter. The pain and joy of adolescence poured onto page after page. My first loss, my first kiss, my first heartbreak, became subjects for stories. I flooded the teen publications with manuscripts, and despite the unpolished writing, the gut reality of the material carried them over the line, and a number of them were published.

And MacKinlay Kantor went on to win the Pulitzer Prize.

Debutante Hill didn't start out as a book, but as a short story called "The Presentation Ball." The idea for the plot came to me one day when I was thumbing through my hometown paper and found a notice on the society page that gave a schedule of events for "this season's debutantes." I couldn't believe what I was reading! A debutante season in a little town like Sarasota, Florida? That town where I had grown up had had one high school with such a small student body that, when I attended it, there had been no dividing line between students from affluent families and poorer ones. Popularity was based upon personality, not social background.

What a gruesome holiday season, I thought, for a girl whose friends were awhirl in the high school social scene, but who, herself, could not make the debutante list! And what a good story idea!

I worked hard on that story and was pleased with the result. I'd decided to have my heroine, Lynn, forbidden to participate in the debutante season because her idealistic father did not feel it was democratic. Understandably, Lynn was resentful, and that resentment grew more intense when her steady boyfriend was drafted to escort the girl whose mother was organizing the ball. The story built to climax with the Presentation Ball, where a series of events helped Lynn regain her sense of values.

The story did not sell. I was bewildered. The situation was interesting and the characters believable. Still, back it came from one magazine after another, even from those who often published my work.

Finally one editor included a note of explanation.

"This is good material," she wrote, "but it just doesn't work as a short story. There is too much here that needs to be further developed. Have you considered writing a book?"

Had I considered writing a book? Yes, of course, I had. It was a dream for some distant day when I was more experienced. What scared me about the thought of tackling a book was the simple fact of its size. A short story might run up to fifteen pages or so, while a book would be over two hundred. How many years would it take to write one, and how could I help but get bogged down along the way?

But that suggestion kept nagging at my mind, and I couldn't seem to let it go.

After all, I reminded myself, I did have a head start. "The Presentation Ball" was seventeen pages. If I cut it in half, I could call it two chapters. Then, if I tacked five chapters onto the beginning and five onto the end, I would have a twelve chapter book. I could do that by starting the book at the time of Lynn's birth, and ending it when she got married.

Such were my thoughts when I purchased a new box of paper and sat down at the typewriter. Such were *not* my thoughts six weeks later when I read the chapters I had written and dropped them into the wastebasket. It took me that long to realize that what I was attempting was not working. Writing a novel by adding onto a short story was just about as feasible as trying to make an evening gown by adding taffeta to the top and bottom of a swimsuit.

There was little that I could add to either the beginning or end of "The Presentation Ball" that would have any bearing on the story, which was about a teenage girl's reaction to a difficult social situation. Anything that happened before that point in Lynn's life, (her childhood, elementary school experiences, summer trips with her family), or afterward, (college, a job, a husband and babies), was superfluous.

The confines of my story were set. I could not make it longer, only larger. And to do that I had to deepen it. The short story had a "plot," a string of related events leading to a single climax. For a book, there would have to be a series of climaxes, each advancing the story and leading Lynn a little further along the road to maturity. Instead of a simple plot, a book must have a theme, and the one I decided upon was; "A year of difficult social change, although at first deeply resented, opens a girl's eyes to ways of life other than her own and helps her mature into a better person." Since the Presentation Ball was only one incident in the development of the theme, I changed the title of the novel to *Debutante Hill*.

I knew now what it was I was trying to accomplish; my next problem was how to accomplish it. How could Lynn's difficult year change her radically as an individual? To work this out, I asked myself some questions: If Lynn can't take part in the social activities in which her friends are involved, what does she do with her time? Does she sit home and brood? Does she make friends with girls who have not been selected for the debutante list? What is Lynn's reaction when her steady is drafted to escort a deb to the parties? Does she retaliate against him or against her parents? If so, how? Does she attach herself, perhaps, to another boy, one she knows her parents won't approve of?

When I reached this point, I'd become so interested in what was going to happen next that I could hardly bear to leave the typewriter long enough to go to the bathroom. That was when I knew the story was working.

It took me close to a year to turn "The Presentation Ball" into *Debutante Hill*. When I stood, at last, with my impressively bulky manuscript in my hands, I realized that I had never enjoyed writing so much, largely because the expanded framework of a novel had given me a chance to develop my characters. In "The Presentation Ball" I'd had Lynn's father state simply, "No, you may not be part of this debutante thing. It's ridiculous." In *Debutante Hill*, I'd had the leeway to present this man in depth so that the reader could know the "why" behind his attitude.

Another character who appeared briefly and insignificantly in the short story was Lynn's sister, Dodie. The reader was told only that Lynn and Dodie had little in common and did not get along. In the book there had been room to develop Dodie as a person, to see her in rivalry with her sister, to hear their arguments, to study their contrasting reactions to a variety of situations. As Lynn matured during the course of the year, we saw the two girls begin to grow closer. Lynn's gradual acceptance of her sister had become a mark of her own change of character. Even though it was a subplot, it had furthered the main theme.

I entered the manuscript in "The Seventeenth Summer Literary Competition," a contest for first-time novelists, held by Dodd Mead & Company. To my astonished delight, it not only won first prize—$1,000 (which was like $50,000 back then), hard-cover and paperback publication, and serialization in a popular magazine—but the contract contained an option to publish my next young adult novel.

My next novel! I couldn't wait to get to the typewriter and roll in a new sheet of paper to start on a book that I planned to call *The Middle Sister*.

Like Lynn in my story, I now knew my true identity.

No longer was I just "a writer." *I was an author!*

— **Lois Duncan**, July 2013

1

"Lynn! Hi, Lynn, wait for me!"

"Hi, Nancy! I didn't see you back there." Lynn Chambers turned with a smile for the bright-haired girl behind her. "In fact, I almost stopped at your house on the way by, but I thought you'd probably left for school already. You were always such an early bird last year."

The September wind, still warm but with the faintest hint of autumn, whipped past the two girls, swirling Lynn's plaid skirt around her legs and mussing the blonde hair that had recently been so carefully combed. The result was that she looked prettier than ever. There was something about Lynn Chambers, a fineness of bone, an ease of bearing, a graceful, unconscious little lift of the head, that made newcomers to Rivertown, who had never seen her before, nod approvingly and ask, "Who is that?"

And whichever long-time resident was asked would usually know.

"That's the older Chambers' girl," he would say. "Nathan Chambers' daughter. You know Dr. Chambers—they live on the Hill."

"Oh, yes, of course."

Even if someone did not know of Dr. Chambers, everyone in Rivertown knew about the Hill. The Hill Road ran at an easy slope down to the river, and along it lived the society families of Rivertown—in lovely homes, one above another, surrounded by spacious yards and green lawns with gardeners to cut them and shade trees and beds of flowers. Rivertown was proud of the Hill and of the people who lived on it And Lynn Chambers represented it perfectly— tall and slim, clear-eyed and gracious, with a touch of un- conscious aloofness with people who did not know her well.

There was nothing aloof about her now, though, as she waited for Nancy Dunlapp to catch up with her.

"Maybe I was early last year," Nancy said wryly, falling into step with her friend, "but there's nothing to get there early for now. Not with that brother of yours away at col- lege." She smiled when she said it, but she could not hide the touch of loneliness underneath. Nancy Dunlapp and Ernie Chambers had gone steady for three years now, ever since she was a freshman and he a sophomore. They were seldom seen apart, the girl with the red hair and the quiet dark-eyed boy. And now Ernie was at college, and Nancy, alone, looked oddly small and incomplete.

Lynn reached over and gave her friend's hand a quick squeeze.

"Don't worry, Nan, December's only three months off. With this being senior year and everything, time will pass before you know it."

"I certainly hope so," Nancy said. "It's terrible how much you can come to depend on somebody, that is, some- body you really care for. You can't imagine—oh, but then of course you can. I keep forgetting that Paul is at college, too." "Oh, it's not the same," Lynn said quickly, trying to shut off the tremor that rose within her at the sound of

Paul's name. "After all, you and Ernie have been a steady team for three years now. With Paul and me, it has only been since last winter."

"Maybe so," Nancy said teasingly, "but I must say he looked pretty solemn when he and Ernie left together, as though he wanted to say, 'To heck with college! I'm going back to high school for another senior year with Lynn.'"

She laughed, and Lynn did, too, but the latter's hand stole to the front of her blouse. Under it, she could feel the thin gold chain which held Paul's class ring. It felt odd still, having the light pressure around the back of her neck and the weight of the heavy ring against her chest, but it was a good feeling too, a warm, secure feeling. It brought back Paul's words when he came by to pick up Ernie and to say a final good-by.

"You take care of yourself," he had said awkwardly, while Ernie was busily piling his suitcases in the back of Paul's car. "You won't have me around to steer you across streets and things, you know."

"I know," Lynn said, fighting down the sting of tears in her eyes.

I won't cry, she told herself firmly, I just won't. But the tears were dangerously close to the surface when she turned to smile up at Paul.

He was smiling, too, a forced smile. And then suddenly, they were both laughing, for the smiles had been so ridiculously inadequate.

Paul reached forward and caught her hand.

"Lynn, I have something for you."

And then she felt the ring, heavy and hard and warm from his finger.

"Your ring!" she whispered. "Your class ring! Paul, how can we—"

"We can't," Paul said. "Not to mean 'going steady' the way it did in high school. I wouldn't ask that when I'm not going to be here to take you to things. But it can mean something else. That is, if you want it to."

"What?" Lynn asked, almost afraid to hear his answer because she knew what it was she wanted so much to hear.

"That you're my girl. That we've got something between us worth hanging onto. That—oh, darn it, Lynn, you know what I'm trying to say."

Lynn nodded, letting her fingers curl around the ring.

"Yes, I know. And I feel that way, too, Paul. I want your ring. It will give me something to kind of hang onto, as you say. Maybe I won't miss you as much."

"Well, you'd better miss me *some*," Paul exclaimed, "or I'm coming back for that ring in a week's time!"

He grinned, and Lynn did, too, and at that moment Ernie turned back from the car.

'Well, are you two through with the fond farewells? Because I've got a girl of my own to say good-by to before we take off."

"I know," Lynn said, "and she's probably about to burst by this time. She told me she was going to be out in the front yard, waiting, at eight o'clock and I think it's closer to a quarter of nine. She'll be sure you've forgotten her."

"No, she won't," Ernie said easily. "Nancy knows better than that."

They are so sure of each other, Lynn thought, so completely sure. But then, Paul and I are, too, now—now that he's given me his class ring.

Ernie gave her a brotherly hug and climbed into the car.

"I've already said my good-bys to the family. Come on, old man, let's get going. I'll look the other way, if you want to make the grand gesture."

"You're a noble guy," Paul said. He turned back to Lynn, but he did not kiss her. She did not expect him to. Paul was not the kind of boy who made a show of things in public. He simply held her hand a moment and then released it and gave her chin a little tap.

"Chin up. I'll be back soon. Don't you lose that ring now; it took my whole allowance for three months straight."

"I won't lose it," Lynn promised. "I'll never lose it!"

And then, sooner than it seemed possible, they were gone.

Now, walking along beside Nancy toward the high school, the whole world had a kind of emptiness about it Last year, she had started toward school in the morning with an excitement burning inside her, with the knowledge that "in just ten minutes . . . seven minutes . . . four minutes . . . I'll see Paul." He would be waiting there by the front steps, maybe talking to some of the boys, for Paul always had friends around to talk to, but his eyes would be wandering off in the direction of the Hill Road, watching for Lynn. Or sometimes she would get there first and watch for him to come. It did not matter which way it happened.

But this year it won't be either way, Lynn thought as the street turned and the building came into view. It's going to seem so lonely!

Nevertheless, there were plenty of greetings as the two girls approached the building. Rivertown High was a public school, but all the young people from the Hill went there.

Occasionally, some family would decide to send their children to a private school, but that was not the usual procedure, for the high school was a good one. Of course, other people went there, too, but the Hill crowd was a crowd of its own, set a little apart from the rest of the students.

It was not a conscious snobbery, and there were members of the Crowd who did not live on the Hill. Most of them had become part of the Crowd because of Paul. Paul had been president of the senior class and captain of the football team, and he had been friends with almost everyone in school. Paul was the sort of boy whom everybody liked, probably because he himself liked everyone.

Lynn had known about him for years before she met him. He was only a year ahead of her, but somehow, during the first years of high school, they had just seemed to miss each other.

"As though," Lynn said later, "every time I came in a door, you walked out one. We were in all the same places, but not at the same time. Just think, we might never have had a chance to know each other at all if it wasn't for Ernie!"

It was through Ernie that she had really come to know Paul.

It was Ernie's junior year, and he was trying out for the football team. Paul was already a member of the team and rumor had it he was the choice for next year's captain. But then Paul was the football type, broad-shouldered and stocky, and Ernie was slender in the same way Lynn was.

Why he wanted to make the team, his parents could not see.

"Really, dear," Mrs. Chambers had said gently, "it's not necessary to go out for something like that, just because a lot of the other boys do. We're not all meant for the same things."

"Sure," his father had agreed. "You're going to be a doctor. That's something most of those muscle-bound fellows could never dream of doing. You don't have to prove yourself by playing football, Son; there are plenty of other ways."

But Ernie had been stubborn. Lynn thought she knew why. It had something to do with getting a letter sweater to present to Nancy. It was just when his steady dates with Nancy were beginning, and he wanted to give her a sweater, as all the boys did when they went with a girl.

"Which is silly," Lynn had declared. "Nancy isn't the kind of girl to care about something like that. She cares about you, not about some old letter."

"Mind your own business, Sis," Ernie had said, not unkindly. "This is something I've made up my mind to do, and I'm going to do it."

And so he practiced. He practiced and practiced—and came home grimy and lame and bruised. Then the day of the tryouts came, and he did not make it He did not say much when he came home that day. He just said, "I didn't make it," and went upstairs and shut himself in his room.

Nancy phoned later, and he would not come to the phone to talk to her, which was unheard of for Ernie. He did not even come out for dinner.

Then, that evening, Paul arrived.

Dodie saw him first. Dodie was a year younger than Lynn and always saw everything.

"It's the Kingsley boy," she exclaimed, glancing out the window, "the Big Wheel of the school! My goodness, don't tell me he's come a'courting!"

"He certainly hasn't if it's me you're considering," Lynn said in equal surprise. "I've never even talked to him."

She went to the door and let Paul in, liking him right away; liking the easy way he walked and the warm blue eyes and the way one eyebrow went up a little higher than the other when he talked.

He said, "I came by to see Ernie."

"Ernie—" Lynn hesitated, wondering what to say. "Ernie's upstairs. He—he's not feeling awfully well. He tried out for the football team today and he—"

"I know," Paul broke in. "I was there. That's what I wanted to talk to him about." He glanced at the stairs. "Do you think it would be all right if I just went on up?"

"Why, yes," Lynn said. "I think that would be fine. It's the first door on the left."

She and Dodie stood in the hallway, watching him mount the stairs and turn down the upstairs hall. They heard him give a sharp rap on a door.

"Why did you let him go up?" Dodie whispered accusingly. "Ernie's going to be furious! You know he doesn't want to see anybody, even Nancy."

"I know," Lynn said. "But I have a feeling Paul's different. I think he'll want to see Paul."

The boys were upstairs for a long time, and when they finally came down together, Ernie had a smile on his face.

"Paul saw me at the tryouts," he said. "He thinks I've got the stuff for the team; I just haven't had practice enough. He's going to work out with me some this year, and next year I'm going to make it."

"Fine!" Lynn replied, glancing gratefully at Paul. "I'm sure you will, too."

Ernie said, "We're going to pick up Nancy and go to a drive-in for a hamburger. Want to come along, Sis?"

"Which sis?" Dodie asked.

"Not you, small fry," Ernie told her. "Big sis."

Lynn said, "Well, I—"

She glanced at Paul. He was smiling at her.

"I wish you would."

"Well, all right. I'd love to."

And that is the way it had begun, quickly, easily, simply—because Paul was the kind of boy who would go out of his way to help somebody who was having a tough time, and because Lynn happened to be there, and maybe because the hamburgers had been a little overdone and they had laughed together about them, and there had been stars, and the River Road, when they drove back, had been drenched in moonlight. Not one thing alone, but all of them, had added up to the fact that it was a special night, and when it was over Paul had asked, "What about next Friday? Want to go to a movie or something?" and Lynn had answered, "Yes." The next year, Ernie had made the football team. And by that winter, Lynn and Paul were going steady.

Because Paul was as he was, easy and cordial and quick to like everyone, he picked up friends everywhere he went, and, through their friendships with Paul, several "outsiders" were drawn into the Crowd. But generally speaking, the little group that sat on the left side of the front steps and called out greetings to Lynn and Nancy as they came up were from the Hill.

"Hi there, you two!" somebody shouted "We were wondering where on earth you were. We've already been through 'who's been where' this summer and have a brand-new topic."

"Well, goodness," Lynn exclaimed, joining the laughing group, "we *are* behind on things! Catch us up."

"Guess what!" Holly Taylor cried, catching Lynn's hand and drawing her down onto the steps. What is the most exciting thing you can imagine happening in Rivertown? To us, I mean!"

"The most exciting thing?" Nancy joined the discussion. "I can't imagine. Maybe Hollywood talent scouts have discovered the beauties at Rivertown High and are planning to make a movie hen, or the school has decided to give flying lessons during gym class, or—"

"Oh, more exciting than that!" Joan Wilson exclaimed. "I'd keep on making you guess, but the bell will ring soon and then we won't have time left to hash it all over. We're going to make our debuts!"

"Our debuts!" Lynn's eyes opened in amazement. "What on earth—"

"We knew you'd be surprised!" Everyone began to talk at once. "We just learned it today. Mrs. Peterson is behind it of course, and it's going to be the most fabulous thing . . . you can't imagine . . . parties every weekend, and a whole week of them during Christmas vacation ... a huge Presentation Ball in the spring..."

"Slowly!" Nancy fairly shouted above the excitement "Please, please, one at a time! Lynn and I want to digest this thing. Suppose just one person tells it."

"Well, I will," Holly Taylor said quickly, "because I heard about it first Mrs. Peterson was talking to Mother on the phone, and she's got the whole thing organized already. It's the first time there have ever been debutantes in Rivertown! Twenty girls have been selected, invitations were mailed last night, and they are going to start things off by being the town's very first debs. All their friends and families will have parties for them during the year, and at Christmas there will be a whole week of big dances, just for them and their escorts. And in the spring, there will be a great ball, with everyone chipping in toward a big name orchestra. Everyone will be presented—" She ran out of breath. "It will be just fabulous," she ended.

"Dances all Christmas vacation!" Nancy echoed happily. "Why, then Ernie will be home for them. How super!" She turned eagerly to Lynn. "Paul will be home, too!"

"Yes," Lynn said, her own excitement beginning to rise. "It does sound marvelous. But how do you know which girls were selected? Who is doing the selecting?"

"Mrs. Peterson, I suppose," Joan Wilson answered. "Since she's the one behind it all. But she—well, it sounds awful to say it this way, but there are really just a certain group of girls she *can* select. What she wants is to start a debutante tradition, a sort of 'entrance-into-society' thing, the way they have in Boston and Atlanta and places like that. So she's got to choose girls from the Hill."

Lynn nodded, accepting the fact without question.

"I suppose so. Twenty. Well, that takes in all of us, I guess and a few others besides."

"Of course, Brenda Peterson will be one," Nancy said.

They were all silent a moment. Then Holly said, "Well, of course. Mrs. Peterson wouldn't be doing it at all, if it weren't for Brenda."

Somewhere a bell rang. The sound filled the air, and instantly the steps became alive with people. The girls scrambled to their feet, momentarily deserting the subject of the debuts.

"Let's try to get seats beside each other in home room this year," Nancy said, catching Lynn's arm.

The crowd swept them forward, through the open doors into the huge central hallway. The smell of the high school rose up around them—books and chalk and desks and people and, somehow, the faint odor of chewing gum. It was a familiar smell, and to Lynn it brought back three years of memories.

When I walked down this hall the last time, she thought nostalgically, Paul was walking beside me, carrying my books, and we were both laughing because school was out and we had the whole long summer in front of us. And now summer is already over, and Paul is at college, and I'm back again without him.

Suddenly, from close behind her, there came a whistle, clear and intimate, and a low voice said, "Well, Miss Chambers! A good-looking gal, but snooty as ever!"

Lynn whirled to find herself looking into the mocking eyes of a dark-haired boy with a thin face and a sarcastic curl to the corner of his mouth.

With an angry toss of her head, she turned away again without bothering to speak.

The boy laughed, a hard little laugh, and swung off down the hall.

"Who on earth—" Nancy began, trying to see who had spoken.

"Oh, it's just that horrid Dirk Masters," Lynn told her disdainfully. "If he isn't the crudest, coarsest thing I've ever seen! Imagine one of the boys from the Hill saying something like that!"

"You were right not to answer him," Nancy said. "I hear he got in some trouble with the police this summer, he and some of the tough bunch of older fellows he goes around with. It's too bad, because Anne is a nice girl."

"Who, his sister?" Lynn looked surprised. "How do you come to know Anne Masters?"

"She had a locker near mine last year," Nancy explained. "I didn't really know her, but we did say 'hello' to each other every day, and she seemed like a sweet little thing, not at all like Dirk. She was in my algebra class, too, and made good grades. It's funny, because I hear Dirk's always flunking everything."

"I guess so," Lynn said, "if he's still in high school. He must be eighteen at least."

Another bell rang.

"Come on," Lynn urged, giving her friend's arm an impatient little tug, "let's not be late to home room our very first day."

Nancy fell into step beside her.

"You know," she confided, "I'm glad to be back. I thought I would be just miserable, coming back to high school without Ernie. We've been going together so long, I didn't see how I'd ever feel right coming back without him. But I do. I mean, I miss him, but still I feel as though the year is going to be fun."

"Yes," Lynn agreed, "and being debutantes will be the saving thing! Isn't it wonderful they thought it up this year? Just think, if they had waited until one year later, we would have missed it, because we'll be away at college then."

And somehow, even without Paul to share it with her, senior year rose up before Lynn, interesting and different and exciting.

2

When Lynn got home from school that afternoon, Dodie was already there, curled up on the porch steps, eating an apple.

Lynn looked at her with surprise.

"What are you doing, just sitting there? Don't tell me Dorothy Eloise Chambers has taken to daydreaming!"

Dodie made a quick face at the sound of her hated name.

"Of course not, silly; I'll leave that to the love-struck members of the family. I'm waiting for Janie. She's been to Nassau during the summer, and her parents bought her a whole collection of records there. She's bringing them over this afternoon." She raised her eyes and gave her sister a penetrating look. "I know what you're going to ask now. 'Is there any mail?'"

Lynn fought down her irritation. Even on days when everything was going perfectly, Dodie had the power to drive her practically insane.

"Well, is there any?"

"Yes," Dodie answered, leaning back on the step and taking another bite of apple. "You got two epistles—one from darling Paul and one that looks like your deb invitation. At least, it's in a shiny white envelope with the Peterson address on the back."

Lynn paused on her way into the house.

"How did you know about the debutante business? It's just being started."

"Maybe so," said Dodie, finishing her apple with one huge bite and tossing the core over the porch railing, "but it's all over school already. They say almost everybody on the Hill is going to 'come out.' Some of the boys are even calling it Debutante Hill and saying you should hang lanterns up and down and have the Presentation Ball right in the middle of the Hill Road."

She stood up quickly, with a sudden, catlike motion. Dodie was not built like the other two Chambers children. Whereas Ernie and Lynn were both tall and slender, with a graceful quality about them, Dodie was small and supple and animated. On first glance, she did not seem as pretty as Lynn, for there was a sharpness to her that her sister did not have, but when she was with people she liked and wanted to have like her, she had a charm that was all her own. Almost everyone liked Lynn. Fewer people liked Dodie, but the ones who did thought she was absolutely wonderful.

"Where is the mail?" Lynn asked now.

"Oh, around some place," Dodie replied helpfully. She glanced down the street and caught sight of Janie. "Hi there! My, what a pile of records! You must have bought out Nassau."

Lynn sighed and turned to go into the house.

Everyone always said, "How nice it must be for you to have a sister just a year younger; somebody to share everything with!"

Well, it would be nice, Lynn thought, if only that were

the way it was. But it isn't—not with Dodie. We have hardly anything in common.

Pausing in the hall, she caught sight of a little pile of mail on the table. Thumbing through it, she quickly located the two letters that were addressed to her.

She opened the one from Paul first. It was the first letter she had ever received from him, and she gazed half-shyly at the hasty, boyish scrawl which would be all that would represent Paul to her until he returned at Christmas time. It was funny to know and care for someone as much as she did for Paul, and yet have his handwriting such an unfamiliar thing. It was like seeing a part of him she had never seen before, meeting and getting to know him in a different way.

After reading the first paragraph, she sighed in relief, for, strange as the handwriting seemed to her, the letter was Paul all over.

Hi, honey! Here I am. It's a great place, but gee, I miss you. The trip up was a tough one. We drove right on through the night like we said we would, but we still didn't make the time we hoped for because we had a flat tire and then something went wrong with the radiator. We got the tire changed without much trouble, but you should have seen us trying to patch that radiator up with chewing gum, especially since neither Ernie nor I can stand the darned stuff. There we were, chewing away, with these awful expressions on our faces. People who passed by must have thought we were crazy.

Ern and I have a room together. Not much to it except a couple of beds and a desk. Ernie already has Nancy's picture stuck on his side of the desk, and my side looks pretty empty. Why not help me fill it by sending me a picture of *my* girl?

Lynn smiled and turned over the page. It was nice that Paul wrote such a good letter. It made him seem closer somehow. She read with interest his account of the first days of classes, of the beanies the freshmen had to wear, of the piles of books which were now residing on the shelf beside his bed.

The letter ended:

How's my ring doing? What I said the day we left—I meant it, you know. I miss you so darned much. Love— Paul.

After the heavier envelope, the small white one beside it felt as though it could not contain a thing. It did, however. As Dodie had anticipated, it was the exciting invitation. Lynn Chambers was being officially invited to participate, as a Rivertown debutante, in the Presentation Ball in the spring and in all the parties and festivities leading up to it during the year.

It will be fun, Lynn thought happily, sliding the card back into the envelope and dropping it into her skirt pocket. She felt like showing it to someone, but her father was at his office and her mother did not seem to be around, either. Wandering into the kitchen, Lynn found out from Rosalie, who was busily peeling carrots for dinner, that Mrs. Chambers was at a Hospital Auxiliary meeting.

Dodie was in her room with Janie, playing records. Lynn could hear them laughing together as she passed the door, but there was no sense of breaking in to show the invitation to Dodie. She knew all about it already.

Stopping at the second-floor telephone, Lynn called Nancy. "Hi! Did your invitation come?"

"Sure did! Impressive, aren't they! And I got a letter from Ernie, too."

"Swell! My family will be burned up when they hear that. They haven't even had a postcard from him."

The two girls chatted for about twenty minutes and then Nancy rang off because she wanted to wash her hair before dinner. Lynn replaced the receiver and wandered aimlessly into her bedroom. She decided to begin a letter to Paul.

She had nearly finished it when Rosalie announced that dinner was ready.

There were candles on the dinner table. It was one of the few things that Mrs. Chambers insisted upon, and, although her father scoffed at it, Lynn thought it a lovely custom. It gave the dining room warmth and grace and a kind of old-time charm. Beneath his laughing protests, she knew her father liked it, too.

The rest of the family was already at the table when Lynn slid into her seat. Her mother turned to her with a smile.

"Well, how was the first day of school? How does it feel to be a senior?"

"Not too different from being a junior," Lynn admitted. "One thing is going to be different, though. Your daughter is not only a senior this year; she is going to be a debutante."

"A debutante!" Her father looked up at the words. "I haven't heard anything about this."

"No," Lynn said, laughing at the surprise on his face, "and I hadn't either until today. Mrs. Peterson is organizing it. They told me about it at school, and then the invitation came this afternoon." She pulled the small white envelope from her pocket and slid it across the table, then turned to help herself from the plateful of rolls Rosalie was serving. "Sounds like it's going to be a lot of fun. Nancy will be one, too."

Her father read the invitation and handed it, wordlessly, to her mother.

Mrs. Chambers read it and laid it aside, saying, "This is a brand new thing, isn't it? I don't think I've ever heard of a debutante in Rivertown before."

"It sounds like something," Dr. Chambers growled, "that that foolish Peterson woman would come up with."

"Why, Daddy," Lynn exclaimed in amazement, "you sound as though you don't like the idea!"

"I don't," her father said shortly. "There's enough class consciousness in this town already without starting something like this."

Lynn was too surprised to answer. She turned to her mother.

"Mother—"

"It does sound like Mrs. Peterson," Mrs. Chambers said slowly. "She's such an organizer. I suppose, being from Philadelphia and all that, she feels that making a debut is about the most important thing in a girl's life. She probably doesn't want Brenda to miss the experience."

"Brenda!" Dodie snorted disdainfully from her side of

the table. "Brenda Peterson is a class 'A' drip, and no debut is going to make her anything else."

Mrs. Chambers shook her head disapprovingly at her younger daughter. "Dodie, that's a horrid way to talk! You don't really know the Peterson girl. After all, she's in Lynn's class, not yours."

"I don't care whose class she's in," Dodie said decidedly. "She's a drip and everybody in school knows it. Why, she wouldn't be invited to anything if they didn't live at the top of the Hill and her mother wasn't head of every woman's club in town."

"Mrs. Peterson *is* the head of a lot of things," Mrs. Chambers admitted. "But I doubt that that makes a difference to the other young people."

"Well, it does," Dodie insisted. "Doesn't it Lynn?"

Lynn nodded. "Yes, I suppose it does. Brenda *is* a drip, Mother, just as Dodie says. She's not pretty; well, she's not exactly homely either. It's just—" She paused, trying to think of the right words. "If you took her feature by feature and asked yourself, 'is her face all right?' and 'are her legs nice?' and 'does she have good teeth?'—you would have to answer yes. There's nothing wrong with her exactly, but when you add everything up, she just doesn't seem to come out to anything. She's sort of a wish-washy little thing. Nobody really dislikes her, but nobody especially likes her either."

Dr. Chambers looked interested. "She seems to be at all the parties," he commented.

"She almost has to be. Her mother gives parties for her, and we are all asked, so, of course, when we give parties, we have to ask her back. But nobody notices her, once she's there."

"She doesn't have many dates, does she?" Dodie asked. Dodie had only recently begun to go out with boys, and this phase of life interested her especially.

"I don't know," Lynn answered. "I don't think so. To tell the truth, I haven't thought of her enough to notice."

Mrs. Chambers shook her head sadly.

"What a sad situation for a young girl. Mrs. Peterson is such a driving force, I can imagine how she reacts to having a daughter who is—well—"

"A drip," Dodie put in mischievously. "Go ahead and say it, Mother. A drip. It's the only word that will do."

"No, I will not say it," her mother said decidedly. "I will not call the poor little thing a name like that. But I can see how frantic Mrs. Peterson must be to organize a whole debutante system in a town this size, just to bring Brenda forth into society. She probably thinks that making a debut is a magic formula designed to—to—"

Again she hesitated, searching for land words.

'To put wings on caterpillars!" Dodie burst out laughing. "Oh, Mother, don't look so horrified! You can't always say nothing but nice things about everybody."

"And you don't have to go out of your way to make unpleasant comparisons," Mrs. Chambers said quietly. "Dodie, that sharp tongue of yours is not your most appealing asset."

Lynn turned back to her father, changing the subject. "You didn't mean it did you, Daddy, about not liking the idea of my making a debut? Everybody is going to be doing it."

"Everybody in Rivertown?"

"No, of course not but all my good friends are—Nancy

and Holly and Joan, oh, all the girls on the Hill. It will be just 'the thing' this year."

"It may be 'the thing,'" Dr. Chambers said slowly, "but that doesn't make it right. It's something I don't like to see starting. There is already a disturbing quality growing in this town, a separating of the people according to where they live and how much money they have, a feeling that doesn't belong in a place of this size. It's bad enough when it exists among the adult population, but it's a tragedy to carry it down into the schools. A public school should be a mixing place, an opportunity for all the young people of the town to get to know each other."

"But having debutantes wouldn't change anything!" Dodie exclaimed. "The kids from the Hill go around together anyhow, so what's the difference whether they make debuts or not?"

Dr. Chambers turned to Lynn. "Is that so? Are all your friends from the Hill?"

"Well, most of them, I guess," Lynn admitted. "We just sort of seem to have more in common, so we go around together."

"Then this debutante setup is worse than I thought," her father said quietly. "It's going to set the dividing line and make it official. It looks to me as though this Peterson woman is going to put the final touch on destroying what might have been a very nice town."

Lynn stared at her father in horror, not believing her ears. "You mean you're not going to let me make my debut!"

Dr. Chambers shook his head. "I'm sorry, Lynn. I just can't go along with it."

Lynn turned helplessly to her mother. "Mother, you

don't agree with him, do you? Talk to him—make him see—"

"I'm sorry, dear," Mrs. Chambers said slowly, "but this is something for your father to decide."

"But, why?" Lynn cried. "Don't you see what this will mean? All my friends are going to be debutantes. There will be all the parties and dances. It's going to last the whole year long. What good is it going to do the town not to have me part of it? They're going to have debutantes anyway. If I decline the invitation, they'll just pick somebody else to take my place."

"Lynn will be out of it all," Dodie chimed in. "It will be like she was in jail or somewhere fenced off. She can't go to anything!"

Lynn was momentarily surprised at her sister's ardent defense. Then she realized that Dodie was probably looking further ahead, to the next year, when she herself would be a senior and eligible to be a debutante.

"I *am* sorry," Dr. Chambers said. "I don't want to make you girls unhappy, but I feel very strongly about this. It is something of which I do not approve. I am going to fight it every step of the way, and I can't very well talk publicly against it if my own daughter is part of it."

Lynn's eyes filled with angry tears.

"But, Daddy—"

Her mother leaned forward, placing a warning hand on her tense fingers.

"All right, Lynn, I think that's enough discussion for the moment. Let's drop the whole thing for now. You and your father both think it over, and we'll talk about it again in the morning."

After she had excused herself from the table, Lynn went upstairs to her room and picked up her letter to Paul. It was practically complete, but she sat down at her desk and added another page, telling him about the dinner table discussion and about her father's attitude.

She wrote bitterly:

It's not fair. It's just not fair. You know what it would mean, Paul; that we couldn't go to anything during Christmas vacation! Not anything! That's when all the big dances will be, and then the Presentation Ball in the spring, and you would be home for that, too!

She wrote on, becoming more and more angry. When she finished, she folded the pages, put them into an envelope and wrote Paul's college address on the front. Then she sealed it and went downstairs to find a stamp.

She paused at the door to the living room, seeing her mother alone, watching television.

"Has Daddy gone out?"

Her mother looked up. "Yes, dear he has gone out on an emergency call. One of the Turner children fell on the stairs. Her mother called in a panic; she says the child can't seem to move her legs."

Lynn exclaimed, "The poor little thing!" Having a doctor for a father, she was used to hearing about accidents and injuries, but their constant occurrence never served to make them less frightening and heartbreaking. "And the poor mother," she added. "She has a lot of children, doesn't she? I think there is a Turner boy in Dodie's class, and I saw him after school the other day, shepherding a whole flock of little ones."

Mrs. Chambers nodded. "I think there are five children. It's a shame, because Mr. Turner was killed in an automobile accident two years ago, and Mrs. Turner is at her wit's end, trying to support the family and take care of the babies at the same time. Yes, Ronnie, the oldest boy, is about Dodie's age, I think. He works at Lawton's Pharmacy after school and in the evenings. That helps some, but it's still rough going for Mrs. Turner, and this latest tragedy isn't going to make it any easier."

Lynn looked at her mother in surprise.

"How do you know all that about the Turners? Surely, Mrs. Turner isn't the sort of person who would be in your bridge club or the Hospital Auxiliary or anything."

"No," Mrs. Chambers said, "I only know about her from your father, who has taken an interest in the family. He was the one who tried to save Mr. Turner after the accident, and later he helped Ronnie get the job at the pharmacy. He says Ronnie is a brilliant boy and a hard worker. Imagine a child that age working all afternoon and all evening to help support his family!"

Lynn said, "He must be a fine person."

Her mother was silent for a moment. When she spoke again, her voice was very serious. "Lynn, you think your father was unfair about forbidding you to be one of the debutantes. Perhaps he was. I doubt whether Nancy Dunlapp's father will forbid Nancy, or Mr. Taylor prevent Holly from joining. But your father is a little different from their fathers, dear, because of his profession. He doesn't just go to business conferences all day and then come to the Hill at night. He sees people, all kinds of people, people like the Turners, and he gets to know them because he takes care of them. He has a chance to see how many good, fine, interesting people there are who don't live exactly the way we do. Ronnie Turner for instance. He would never be invited to one of the debutante dances, but I imagine he is a lot finer person than many of the boys Dodie is beginning to date."

She hesitated, trying to see what impression she was making on her daughter. Finally, when Lynn remained silent she continued, "What Daddy wants, dear, is for you not to separate yourself so entirely from everybody who isn't exactly like you. You need to know and like all kinds of people, if you aren't going to grow up into a—a—" She repressed a smile. "Dodie would love this—into a Mrs. Peterson."

Lynn nodded. "I know; I can see that It's just—oh, Mother, it will be so hard! I'll be shut out of everything!"

"No," her mother said softly. "It may seem that way at first, but you will find, I think, that when some doors are closed to you, others will open. . . . Lynn, when I was a young girl, living in Atlanta, I was one of the charmed so-called 'social set.' I was the most popular debutante of the season, and, if you knew Atlanta society, you would know what that meant. When I met your father, he was an intern at a local hospital. He had worked his way through medical school and was living on nothing but ham sandwiches. My parents could never see how fine and brilliant and ambitious he was. All they could see was that he was not a member of Atlanta 'society.' We eloped, and they never forgave us. They died, still feeling that way."

Lynn's eyes grew larger. "So that's why Daddy feels so strongly about this?"

"Yes," her mother said softly, "that's one of the reasons." Lynn lay awake a long time after she went to bed. It was almost midnight when the door to her room opened softly and she saw her father standing in the doorway. She could not see his face, but by the hall light shining behind him, she could see he was stooped a little, the way he always stood when he was weary.

He whispered, "Are you awake?"

Lynn raised her head. "Yes, Daddy. How is the Turner child?"

"She's going to be all right." Her father did not come into the room. He merely stood there, looking at her. He did not say things easily. Finally he said, "About our conversation tonight; I've been thinking it over. If it means so much to you, Lynn—well—"

"That's all right," Lynn assured him. She heard her voice saying it, as though it were someone else's voice. "That's all right Mother and I talked about it. I—I can see that you're right."

"No hard feelings?"

"No hard feelings."

He looked so tired, standing there in the doorway, his shoulders sloped forward, his head bent a little.

Lynn relaxed on her pillow and said something she had not said for a long long time.

"I love you, Daddy."

Dr. Chambers did not answer at once. When he did he said only, "And I you, Daughter." Then he closed the door.

3

Lynn got up the next morning feeling as dedicated, strong and purposeful as a Christian martyr going forth to face the lions. However, by the time she had washed her face, brushed her teeth, dressed and put on lipstick, her purpose was beginning to falter a little. It was fairly easy to be noble at night, in a moment of sentiment, but in the bright light of day, the thought of the morning ahead of her was a little more difficult.

Dodie did not help matters.

"You're crazy," she said at breakfast, helping herself to a handful of toast. "You should never have let Daddy talk you into something like this. I'm darned if anybody's going to talk *me* out of being a debutante next year. I'm going to be the debutantiest one of them all."

"I'll bet!" Lynn said irritably. "Just you wait Daddy will have something to say about it when the time comes."

"He can say what he wants," Dodie declared, "and it won't make any difference. I'll kick and scream and throw things at the walls. Daddy can't hold out against something like that and he wouldn't have held out against you either, if you had stood your ground. You just give in too easily."

Lynn thought of her father the night before, standing in the doorway. He had been ready to give in then. He had said, "If it means so much to you, Lynn—" All she would have had to reply was, "It does, Daddy. It means everything."

But she had not said it. Now she wished she had—but now it was too late. Her decision was made, and she was stuck with it.

Lynn swallowed her orange juice and blotted her mouth carefully with a napkin, so as not to blur her lipstick. "Ready to go?" she asked her sister.

Dodie glanced at her watch. "You go ahead. I told Janie I'd stop by her house and walk over with her."

"Janie!" Lynn exclaimed with an impatience not natural to her. "Janie, Janie, Janie! You two are inseparable. What do you see in her, anyway? I mean, she may be a nice enough girl, but you and she can't have much in common. You're a straight A student and I hear she flunked both her language courses last year."

"She won't this year," Dodie said. "I'm going to tutor her."

Lynn shook her head in bewilderment. Dodie never ceased to surprise her. Everything she did seemed out of character. It was difficult to imagine sharp-tongued Dodie sitting down patiently to tutor somebody in Latin. Sometimes Lynn felt that she did not understand her younger sister at all.

The walk to school was a long and lonely one. The year before, she had always walked with Ernie and Nancy, but now Ernie was away and, somehow, she had missed Nancy. Evidently her friend had left too late or too early for her to intercept her on the way. She caught sight of some of the other girls from the Hill, walking ahead of her, but she was in no hurry to call out to them.

They will have received their deb invitations, Lynn thought bitterly, and that's all they will want to talk about.

She sighed and walked on alone, arriving at school just as the first bell rang.

It was not until lunch time that she had a chance to draw Nancy aside and confront her with the bad news.

"I'm not going to be one of the debutantes this year."

"You're not!" Nancy stared at her in amazement. "Lynn Chambers, what on earth are you talking about? Why, you were telling me on the phone just yesterday afternoon that you received your invitation."

"I know I did," Lynn said. "But that was before I told my parents. Daddy doesn't want me to make a debut."

"He doesn't!" Nancy's disbelief was slowly changing to horror. "You mean, you can't be part of it all? How perfectly horrid! Why would he say a thing like that? How can he be so mean?"

"He's not mean," Lynn said shortly, surprising herself at her immediate loyal defense of her father. "He doesn't approve of debutantes, so he doesn't want me to be one. That's all there is to it."

Nancy gave her friend's hand a sympathetic squeeze. "Well, try not to worry about it Lynn. Maybe he'll change his mind when he sees that everybody else from the Hill is going to be in on it and when he sees how much fun we're having and everything."

"Maybe," Lynn said, knowing that he would not. Once her father's mind was made up, nothing short of an earthquake was going to change it.

By the time she had filled her tray at the cafeteria and seated herself at a table, Lynn found that everyone knew.

She did not have to tell anyone of her father's decision, for Nancy had spread the word for her, and she was greeted by a wave of sympathy.

"It's tough luck," Holly Taylor declared. "But maybe your dad will come around."

Joan Wilson said, "I don't understand how he could feel that way. Why, my father was delighted! He said he thought it sounded like a wonderful idea and a real social lift for the town."

Lynn murmured something unintelligible and tried to bury her face behind a sandwich. She sat quietly, letting herself fade more and more into the background as the other girls' conversation picked up on all sides and rattled gaily on, from one end of the subject to the other and back again.

"A party each weekend! That's the way the schedule is going to run, and then every day of the holidays. My aunt is going to give my party—a luncheon—and it should be marvelous! Aunt Jenny always has such wonderful new ideas for things."

"Mother's going to plan a dinner dance for us. She says she'll even hire an orchestra!"

"The Christmas parties are going to be the most exciting. All the fellows will be home from college, so we'll have more boys than we know what to do with."

"Daddy says my big Christmas present this year will be a new dress for every Christmas party!"

They were all talking at once—Joan, Holly, Nancy—the whole table full of girls. And down at the end, Lynn saw to her surprise, was Brenda Peterson, her mousy little face flushed with excitement.

She's part of it, Lynn thought, with an anger out of all

proportion to the situation. She couldn't get to be one of the gang any other way, so now her mother is buying her way in by organizing this debutante program.

She had never before felt anything personal against Brenda Peterson. Now, watching her shy smile and the way she leaned forward eagerly to join the conversation, she felt a sudden, strong dislike.

Glancing past Brenda to the next table, Lynn saw another group of girls quietly eating. They were not the Hill girls, but there were one or two of them whom she knew fairly well from sitting near them in classes. Rachel Goldman, a dark, attractive girl, had written the winning entry in last year's essay contest. Clara Marivella was president of the square dance club, an organization none of the Hill crowd ever entered. Anne Masters, the girl Nancy had referred to as a "sweet little thing," was telling them something. It must have been something funny, for Rachel and Clara both burst out laughing.

Watching them, Lynn wondered what they were laughing at. She had never really noticed them very much before, but now, suddenly, she saw them as an attractive group of girls who seemed to be living satisfactory lives all their own, with their own friendships, their own jokes, their own laughter.

Anne glanced up, caught Lynn's eyes upon her and smiled. Her smile was natural and friendly and spontaneous, and automatically Lynn smiled back.

She thought, I wonder what Anne Masters is like. It must be hard having a brother like Dirk. I wonder what she could have to say that would be so funny that everyone would start to laugh.

Beside her, Joan was talking. Lynn turned, trying to catch the trend of the conversation.

". . . and so Father said, 'Two hundred dollars apiece is an awful lot to contribute toward one dance.' And Mother said, 'It isn't really, dear, if you knew how much it usually costs for a girl to make a debut. Why, in the big cities, each girl has her own coming-out party, and each one costs thousands of dollars. This way, there will just be one big ball, with everyone contributing toward it and everybody "coming out" at once.' And when Father heard that he said, 'O.K., O.K., I'm not arguing. I think it's a fine idea.' Mother can handle him all right."

Lynn sat quietly, feeling oddly apart, as the wave of laughter swept the table. Then somebody down at the other end began telling about her father's reaction to the debutante invitation. Everyone leaned forward to hear.

Lynn laid her half-eaten sandwich on her plate and got quietly to her feet. Nobody seemed to notice when she did so. Nobody said, "Hi, Lynn, don't go away! Come on and sit down here. It's no fun talking about things unless you're here to hash them over, too." Everyone was intent on the girl at the end of the table.

As she finished her story, laughter broke out again, and this time it was Brenda Peterson who said something, hesitantly, in that bland little voice of hers. Lynn could not hear what it was, but again there was laughter.

With a shrug of irritation, Lynn walked away from the table and out of the cafeteria.

She wandered aimlessly across the schoolyard. Here and there were knots and groups of students, laughing and talking, but none of them were people she knew very well.

In a little group over by the fence, she saw Dodie and her friend Janie and several other girls from their particular junior class branch of the Hill crowd.

Dodie looked up as she passed and started to say something and then, catching the look on her sister's face, evidently thought better of it

Entering the building, Lynn went to her locker and located her Spanish book. There was an empty classroom several doors down. She went in and sat down at one of the desks and began her next day's translation. She had already completed two pages when the bell rang to announce that lunch hour was over.

And that was the way it went, that day and the next and the next.

It's as though I were a stranger, Lynn told herself bitterly. I don't seem to belong any more.

It was not that her old friends were intentionally ignoring her. On the contrary, they were especially pleasant whenever she was with them.

"What a darling dress, Lynn! Where in the world did you get it?"

"That math test was a humdinger, wasn't it! How do you think you did on it?"

"What do you hear from Paul, Lynn? Is he coming home for Thanksgiving or will you have to wait until Christmas?"

It was nice talk, friendly talk, the way it had always been, but there was something missing. The element of spontaneity. They could no longer jabber away in complete ease when Lynn was with them, because the main topic of conversation these days was the first debutante party, to be held the following weekend, at Joan's house. And Lynn would not be there.

"I wish you were coming," Joan said sincerely, giving her friend an apologetic smile. "I feel like a dog, having a party without you, Lynn. Why, it's the first time I can ever remember our doing anything when you weren't right there, the center of everything. It's going to seem awfully flat without you."

"No, it won't," Lynn said lightly. "Not a dinner dance! Why, it will be perfectly marvelous, Joan; it can't help but be."

"I wish you were coming," Joan said again. But she seemed happy enough to turn the conversation to another subject.

As the day of the party grew nearer, Lynn found herself withdrawing more and more from the crowd on one pretext or another and spending her time alone. She deliberately arrived at school after the first bell in the morning, so there was no time to join in the pre-school conversation on the left side of the school steps. She ate lunch quickly at the noon hour and managed to slip away before she could get swept into the lunch table conversation. Once out of the cafeteria, she usually located an empty classroom or went to the library and spent the remainder of the hour studying. During gym class, she dressed quickly and played hard, keeping free from the little groups of girls that gathered to gossip before the mirrors in the dressing room or in clusters under the trees that lined the playing field.

She could give no good reasons for her actions. It was not that she was angry with the girls themselves. She knew they wanted her with them. It was more a feeling of defense.

If she could not be in on everything, then she would rather not be in on anything at all. It was better, much better, to be walking by yourself of your own free will than to be in the midst of a crowd that was concentrated on things in which you could have no part.

Strangely, it was Dodie who sensed this. She did not say much, but once in a while she came out with a remark that surprised Lynn by its perception.

"You can't just cut away completely, you know," she said once, in her sharp way. "Everybody has to belong to something."

And another time— "Are you and Nancy on the outs? I never see you together any more."

"No," Lynn answered shortly, "we're not 'on the outs,' as you so crudely put it. We're just doing different things."

"Oh?" Dodie gave her a keen glance. "Well, I know what Nancy is doing, being neck deep in all this debutante business; but what are you doing? You're not even in the Art Club this year, are you?"

"No," Lynn admitted.

The Art Club was the favorite school club of those from the Hill. Almost everyone belonged, whether he could draw or not, simply because it was the thing to do. The club made posters for school functions, had lecturers in to discuss different forms of art and made trips to museums and art galleries in surrounding towns. Lynn had belonged to it for two years, because, aside from the fun of being with everyone else, she enjoyed art. She liked the trips to art galleries for their own sake, and she herself had a nice knack with a pencil or charcoal. The Art Club had always been a favorite project with her, and the year before she had been its vice-president. This year, she had gone to one meeting. Elections were held. Holly Taylor was elected president; Holly's steady Don Pearce, vice-president; and Brenda Peterson, secretary.

"I don't understand," Lynn had whispered to Nancy with a bitterness she had never felt before. "The person who was vice-president last year is always elected president. It's kind of an unwritten rule."

"I know," Nancy answered uncomfortably. "It's just— well, Lynn, maybe they think you're not as interested in the old crowd as you used to be. You really do seem kind of aloof with everybody these days."

"Well, maybe I do," Lynn said, "but what difference should that make? This is an art club, not a social club. I'm as interested in the art side of the club as I ever was."

She had walked out of the room after the meeting was over with her head high and her eyes defiant. But she had not gone back.

"I'm just not very interested in the club any more," she said to Dodie. "Especially when Brenda Peterson is an officer." Dodie had given her a long, knowing look, but she had not bothered to answer.

It was during one of her lonely lunch periods that Lynn had her first conversation with Anne Masters. She had left the cafeteria early and was entering the school building when Anne spoke to her.

Lynn whirled in surprise.

"What?"

"I said hi," Anne said a little shyly. "I—I wondered how you thought you did on the Spanish quiz."

"Oh, fairly well, I think," Lynn answered. "I've been doing a lot of studying lately."

She turned and looked at Anne. Although she had known the girl casually ever since they had started high school, it was the first time she had really looked at her, and she was a little surprised at what she saw. Anne Masters was not a pretty girl in the accepted sense of the word. She was small and thin, with eyes a little too large in her narrow face and not enough color in her cheeks. But there were other things about her that were quite lovely. There was a clean, honest openness about her face, and a sweet curve to her mouth, and a very feminine daintiness about her movements. She looked back at Lynn and smiled, and there was a quiet friendliness about her that could not be denied.

After a second's hesitation, Lynn came over and sat down beside her on one of the benches in front of the school building.

"How do you think you did?" she asked.

"Oh, passably, but that's all." Anne wrinkled her nose in an amusing little gesture of distaste. "Spanish isn't my strong subject, I'm afraid. It's funny, because with Clara Marivella living down the street from me, I should speak like a native. Her father's always standing in the doorway and calling things to her."

"Is Clara's father Spanish?" Lynn was surprised. "I mean, I knew she had a Spanish name, but I thought it was from way back. I didn't know her father actually spoke the language."

"He and Mrs. Marivella, too," Anne replied. "Clara says they never speak anything but Spanish at home. Sometimes she'll be chatting away with us girls and she'll throw in a

Spanish phrase without even knowing it. She's so used to speaking it at home that she forgets where Spanish starts and English begins."

"How fascinating!" Lynn found, to her surprise, that she was really enjoying the conversation. "Why, think how simple Spanish class must be to her! She probably sits there and—"

"Well, hi." The voice came from close behind her. "Hi, there! Don't tell me the Princess of the Hill deigns to sit here talking to my little sister!"

Dirk Masters stepped around the side of the bench and stood grinning down at them.

Anne glanced up with a flash of anger.

"Dirk, behave yourself! If you can't say something polite to my friends, I'd rather you didn't speak to them at all."

Lynn's eyes widened in surprise. It was amazing to hear this sweet-faced little girl speaking up without an instant's hesitation to the tough, insolent Dirk Masters. She waited breathlessly for his answering burst of anger, but, to her further surprise, none came. Instead, he grinned at his sister with a kind of pride.

"Simmer down, Sis. Regular spitfire, isn't she?" He turned to Lynn. "I hear you're not making your entrance into society. My sister here isn't going to be a debutante either, you know, but not because she doesn't want to. She wasn't invited. Of course, you don't know what it's like not to be invited to something. When *you* turn something down, it's because you don't want it, not because it doesn't want you."

His voice was hard, with a deep bitterness.

Anne said, "Dirk, this is ridiculous. There is no reason

for you to make a scene like this about nothing."

"You think you're so great," Dirk continued harshly. "You and your superior Hill crowd. My sister would make a classier debutante than any of you."

Lynn drew back, feeling her own anger rising to the surface. "You don't have to make your rude, nasty remarks to me, Dirk Masters! If you want to talk about the debutante parties, go talk to Brenda Peterson. Her mother is running them, not mine. I don't have a single thing to do with it."

"And if she did," Anne put in quickly, "it wouldn't be any of your business, Dirk. Why do you always have to be so rude to people?"

Dirk retorted, "I'm not being rude. I'm just being friendly. I've never had a chance to talk to the Princess of the Hill before. It's a shock to see her mixing it up at our level." He turned back to Lynn, a mocking light in his eyes. "Well, Princess, since you won't be going to the debutante party this Saturday, how about you and I painting the town together? Or do you think your Hill crowd would ever speak to you again?"

He was laughing at her, baiting her, putting her in a position where she would have to be rude to him in reply.

How bitter he is, Lynn thought.

She raised her eyes and looked Dirk full in the face. It was a handsome face, in a lean, arrogant sort of way. Like Anne, he was thin, and his features were very much like hers, but there was something else too, a kind of hardness that was completely lacking in Anne. His eyes were dark and mocking, and his hair fell forward over his forehead in a careless, rakish way, as though he did not care enough to push it back.

To Lynn's surprise, she felt her heart begin to beat a little faster.

He is handsome, she thought but so tough and insolent and cocky! How I'd love to take him down a peg or two . . . and I know how to do it.

If she had thought, she would never have done it—not really. It was the kind of thing that was fun to think about and to laugh about with the girls, but never, never actually to do. It was with real surprise that Lynn heard her voice saying, coolly and easily, as though it were the least important thing in the world:

"Why, thank you, Dirk, that would be very nice. I'd love to go out with you Saturday night."

4

When she thought back upon it later, Lynn decided it was worth it, worth every minute of it, just to see the look of shock upon Dirk's face. He had been standing there grinning at her, waiting to see her wriggle and squirm in an effort to be polite and still refuse his left-handed invitation. Her simple words of acceptance took him completely off guard and left him staring at her in bewilderment.

"What?"

"I said thank you, I'd love to go out with you Saturday. What time will you be by for me?"

"Why, I—I—" Dirk's smile was gone now. "I didn't mean—that is, you—you don't really want to go?"

"Of course, I want to go." Lynn said sweetly. She knew she should back out now; it was the perfect moment for it but she was too amused by Dirk's discomfort to let the situation drop. "How about eight o'clock? Do you know where I live?"

"Sure," Dirk said, "I know where you live. But your folks. What will they say? They don't even know me."

"They'll meet you," Lynn said, "Saturday night."

The bell rang, announcing the end of lunch hour and the beginning of afternoon classes. Lynn got to her feet for she knew she could not have continued the conversation a single moment longer without bursting into laughter and ruining the whole effect. Seeing Dirk embarrassed was so completely out of character!

Now she gave him her brightest smile and joined the crowd moving into the building.

It was funny. Terrifically funny then—and it would have been even more so if there had been someone to share it with, but she could think of no one to tell. Nancy, Joan, Holly—they would all be horrified. A date with Dirk Masters! Why, it was as far out of the question as dating Satan himself.

And the more Lynn thought about it, the less amusing it began to seem to her. Yes, she had succeeded in disconcerting Dirk. The last thing in the world he had ever expected was that he would find himself dating Lynn. But a boy like Dirk would resent being put on a spot. If he had been bitter and resentful of her before, what would he be like now?

The question was not a comforting one.

I never should have gone on with it, Lynn thought. Why didn't I slip out while I could? Now I'm committed, and there's not much I can do about it.

She had not meant to mention the date much beforehand at home, but she was forced to because of Dodie who, for the first time in her live, asked her if she wanted to go to the movies.

"It's a good show," she said, "a Western. Good reviews and everything."

Lynn could not believe her ears.

"You want to go to a Western? How come? You never liked them before. And if you do want to go, why aren't you going with Janie?"

Dodie shrugged. "I don't mind a Western once in a while, and I thought you—well, I just thought maybe you'd like to go. It really doesn't matter to me one way or the other."

Lynn thought, did Mother ask her to go to the movies with me Saturday, in order to give me something to do to keep me from thinking about the dinner dance? It was not like something her mother would do. And yet there did not seem to be any other answer. She and Dodie never went to the movies together.

"Thanks," she said now, "but I can't. I've got a date."

"A date?" Dodie said in surprise. "Who on earth are you dating, with Paul away at college and all the eligible fellows at the debutante dance?"

"Dirk Masters."

"Who?" Dodie stared at her in amazement. "You're joking!"

"No," Lynn said, "I'm not joking. I really do have a date with him. Is there any reason why I shouldn't?"

"Why, he's a juvenile delinquent!" Dodie exclaimed. "He's already been in trouble a couple of times with the police. He's wild and he runs around with a terrible crowd. How can you possibly—" Then, suddenly, a look of understanding crossed her face. "Oh, I see what you're doing. You can't date the Hill fellows because they're all at the deb parties, so you'll date the other extreme. Let Daddy meet Dirk once, and he'll be begging you to get back with the old Hill crowd again."

There was admiration in her voice at the cleverness of the plan, but a note of contempt, too.

"It's smart, Lynn, but it doesn't sound like you."

"Why, that wasn't my idea at all!" Lynn protested. But even as she said it, her mind slid along Dodie's words, seeing the possibilities. She had not consciously planned for her date with Dirk to have this effect on her parents, but perhaps it would, at that. And if it did, certainly she would not be sorry.

When Saturday evening finally arrived, Lynn found herself dressing with as much care as she had ever shown on her most exciting date with Paul. She had selected her tan wool dress with the three-quarter length sleeves and gold belt, the dark brown suede pumps with medium high heels. It was a good outfit, simple and striking, and she hoped that Dirk, who had never seen her except in a school dress or a skirt and sweater, would be overwhelmed.

He's always making remarks about my being as snooty as a princess, Lynn thought, brushing her blonde hair back into a shining pony tail. Well, all right, let him see what it feels like to date a princess. I'll be just as gracious and charming as can be, the way a real princess always is with her subjects, but I'm going to dress in good taste and look like the kind of a person I am, not like the flashy girls he's probably used to dating.

She finished dressing just as the doorbell rang.

He's here!

And it was then that Lynn realized that, underneath, she had been half-expecting Dirk to back out of their date. She knew he had not meant for her to accept—that the whole situation was not at all what he wanted. She had not talked to him since he had asked her. She had passed him in the hall every once in a while, but he had always avoided her eyes and never once stopped to speak to her, to confirm their date. So, although she had dressed carefully for this evening and was, for all practical purposes, expecting him to arrive, she would not really have been surprised if he had not.

Now, with the sound of the bell, came the realization— he's here! He's actually here!

And with it came a wave of panic.

It was like nothing she had experienced with Paul. Oh, she had been excited about dating Paul. When Paul rang the bell, she felt a quickening, a leap of happiness, a kind of singing inside. But never panic. Paul, even when she first met him, was dear and familiar because he was very much like Ernie and the boys Ernie went around with. Paul's father and Dr. Chambers were in Rotary together. Paul's mother was in Mrs. Chambers' bridge club. She knew Paul—the kind of places he would take her, the way he would feel about things, the things he would talk about—because they came from the same world.

Dirk did not.

But I can't stay here all night, Lynn told herself firmly, giving herself one last look in the mirror. Tonight may be perfectly horrible, but at least it is just one evening. You can stand anything for one evening. I was foolish to get myself into this, but four hours from now it will be over and I'll never have to look at or speak to him again.

Taking a deep breath, she turned away from the mirror and went downstairs.

Dirk was sitting in the big chair in the living room, talking to Dr. Chambers. He was dressed neatly, Lynn noticed at once, in a good quality sports shirt and freshly pressed slacks. His hair was combed back from his forehead with care. He looked clean and handsome and rather nervous, perched uncomfortably on the edge of the chair, trying to make conversation. When Lynn came in, he looked up in relief.

"Hello!" Lynn swept down the bottom steps with all the princess-like grace she could muster. "How are you, Dirk? I see you've met my father."

"Yes," Dr. Chambers said, rising as his daughter came toward them. "We find we have some acquaintances in common—the Turners. Dirk says they live a few houses down from him."

"Oh?" Lynn gave Dirk a charming smile. "How nice."

Seeing Dr. Chambers rise, Dirk got up too, standing uncomfortably with his hands in his pockets.

"Are you ready to go now?"

"Yes," Lynn said, "all ready."

Her father gave her a pat on the shoulder and held out his hand to Dirk.

"I'm glad to have met you, Dirk. Have a nice evening and drive carefully."

Dirk flushed slightly. "I will, sir. Thank you." Lynn could not remember ever seeing him so subdued.

Once they were out of the house, however, the awkwardness seemed to slide off him and the old Dirk began to reappear. He gave her a flash of the sardonic smile she knew so well.

"You look real neat tonight, Princess! Are all those fancy clothes just for me?"

"You didn't say where we were going," Lynn answered pleasantly, "so I wasn't sure what to wear. I thought this was a happy medium."

"That's right I said 'paint the town' but I didn't say where. Well ..." He hesitated. "What about a movie to start with? There's a good show at the State. Then we can go on from there."

"Fine!"

There was a car parked by the curb. Dirk walked over and opened the door.

"Climb in. Hope this is classy enough for you."

Lynn got in, choking down her surprise. The car was a brand new Chevrolet convertible.

She asked, "Is this yours? It's a beautiful car. I've never seen you drive it to school."

"No, I don't take it to school." Dirk slid into the driver's seat and started the engine. He seemed anxious to change the subject. "Your dad's nice. I thought he'd be different. It's funny, him knowing the Turner kids."

"He's their doctor," Lynn said. "He took care of Mr. Turner while he was alive, and now he takes care of the children. He got the oldest boy a job in a drugstore. He says he's a grand boy."

"Ronnie? Yes, he's a nice enough kid, I guess." Dirk turned the car off the Hill Road and drove toward town. "But he's not very smart."

"Why, Daddy seemed to think he was awfully smart. He makes top grades in school and holds a job and—"

"Oh, sure, he's smart in schoolwork, but that's no test of a guy's brains. There he is, wearing himself out at that darned drugstore every day, all afternoon on weekdays and all day long on Saturdays, and what does he get for it? Thirty dollars a week, maybe. Probably less."

"Well, thirty dollars is thirty dollars," Lynn said. "It sounds fine to me."

Dirk shrugged his shoulders. "It's an awful lot of work for peanuts."

They drove on in silence until they reached the State Theater.

The movie was the Western that Dodie had suggested seeing. The theater was a nice one. Lynn had been there many times with the girls and with Paul, and she automatically turned down the aisle toward the left-hand middle section where the Hill crowd always sat. She was surprised when Dirk caught her arm.

"Come on, let's sit in the balcony."

"In the balcony? Why? You don't see nearly as well there."

"Sure, you do. That's where the gang always sits."

Lynn hesitated and then turned to follow him up the stairs to the balcony. If by 'the gang' he meant the older crowd he seemed to run around with, she would just as soon not sit with them. But after all, she was Dirk's guest and it was up to him to say where they would go. Besides, she was going to be a princess this evening, gracious and charming, or die in the attempt!

Once they reached the balcony, Lynn felt as though she were in a separate world. There was a rustle of people moving as they approached, and somebody called, "Hey, Masters, come sit over here! Who's the chicken tonight?"

Dirk took her arm and steered her down an aisle to a group of seats where some young people were sitting. Straining to see them in the darkened theater, Lynn thought she recognized one of the group as the plump, blonde girl who sat in the last row in English class, but she was not sure. She did not think she recognized any of the others.

Dirk steered her into an empty seat and sat down beside her. To her relief, he did not introduce her with any of his sarcastic remarks. He merely said, "This is Lynn Chambers."

"Lynn Chambers!" Lynn may not have known the crowd, but they seemed to know her. "You mean *the* Lynn Chambers! Well, for crying out loud, Masters, you're mixing with royalty!"

The plump girl gave Lynn a shy smile.

"I'm Greta Burly. You probably don't know me, but I'm in your English class."

"Of course, I know you," Lynn said politely. "You sit in the last row."

The girl beamed. "Why, I never thought you noticed!"

The boy she was with threw an arm around her shoulders and pulled her toward him. "Hey, either concentrate on the picture or on me. Save your female jabber till later."

Lynn turned her own attention to the picture. It was difficult, for despite what Dirk said, the balcony was far from a choice spot for viewing. Everyone in the balcony seemed to be smoking, and within a few minutes, Lynn felt her eyes burning. Behind them, several couples were giggling, and, after a moment, there was a muffed sound that Lynn glance over her shoulder in alarm. She turned back again, her face burning.

Beside her, Dirk chuckled. "What's the matter, didn't you ever see people kiss each other before?"

"Not in public like that," Lynn whispered back scornfully.

"Well, kid, you're learning new things every day."

With an effort, Lynn focused her attention on the

screen and managed to keep it there through the rest of the picture, determinedly ignoring all sounds from the seats behind or to the side of her.

It was a relief when the picture ended and they got up to leave.

"Where are we going now?"

It seemed they were now part of the gang. Everyone assumed they would be going somewhere together.

Someone suggested, "What about Charlie's?"

"O.K., fine."

Dirk said, "I've got a car tonight; we'll meet you over there. Anybody want a ride?"

The boy who was with Greta Burly said, "Sure, we'll ride with you. I want to see that buggy make some time."

They stumbled together down the stairs from the balcony, shoved and trampled by the masses of people moving in the same direction. And then, a few moments later, they were in the car, Greta and her date in the back seat, and Lynn beside Dirk in the front. She said, "Where is Charlie's? I don't think I've ever heard of it."

"It's a good place." Greta said. "It's where all the gang goes."

Dirk swung the car out of the city traffic and onto the River Road. He began to drive fast. The wind sang past the windows. The boy in the back seat gave a crow of delight "Say, this is the greatest! Don't you wish you had a buggy like this?"

But *isn't* it Dirk's? Lynn thought in surprise. She watched the needle creeping across the speedometer with apprehension. Fifty-five . . . sixty . . . sixty-five. She thought, I won't say anything. Greta and her date are in the car just as much as I am. I'm not going to be the one to be a coward about this.

Seventy . . . seventy-five. The wind was a wild shriek on all sides of them.

Lynn glanced beseechingly at Greta in the back seat, but she could not see the girl, only a blur. Then she heard a whisper, a muffled giggle. She realized that Greta and her date were not noticing the speedometer any more; they were too wrapped up in each other.

Lynn turned back to see the needle at the far right of the speedometer. She gave a gasp, all her pride leaving her in a sharp surge of panic.

"Dirk, please! Please slow down! We'll all be killed!"

Dirk glanced down at her. He was grinning.

"Scared, Princess?"

"Yes, I'm scared," Lynn gasped. "Please, please, Dirk, don't be so crazy! You promised Daddy you'd drive carefully. You know you did!"

There was a giggle from the back seat as Greta evidently came up for air long enough to catch this remark.

"He did what?"

"He promised my father he'd be careful driving."

Greta's date leaned forward. "Hey, did you really, Masters? Did the doc sit you down and give you a book of instructions before he let you take his darling daughter out?"

He was laughing, and Greta was too, as though it were the biggest joke in the world.

Lynn felt her face growing hot with fury. She waited for Dirk to come up with a similar remark, but he did not. Instead, to her surprise, he took his foot off the accelerator and let the car coast to a slower speed. Then he turned to the right, into a driveway, and came to a full stop in front of a small lighted building.

"Here we are . . . Charlie's." Dirk threw open his door and got out Lynn waited a moment to see if he was coming around to open hers, and when he did not she opened it herself and climbed out slamming the door angrily behind her.

Of all the rude things, she thought almost as irritated as she had been about the speeding. Why, Paul would never in the world get out of a car and walk off, leaving me to trail along by myself. It's just not the way a boy acts on a date.

Then she realized that Greta too was climbing out of her own side of the car and shutting the door behind her. The two boys were standing together by the front of the car, waiting for the girls to join than.

Lynn felt her anger diminish slightly.

He didn't mean to be rude, she thought. He just doesn't know any better. This must be the way his crowd acts.

As she caught up with him, Dirk took her arm and steered her through the door into the place known as Charlie's.

The moment she was inside, Lynn knew it was not the kind of place she ought to be in. Charlie's was a bar, purely and simply, and did not even pretend to be anything else. There was a juke box playing in one comer, a long counter lined with stools, and a row of booths around the outside. There were several people at the counter, and three of the booths were filled. The far booth, over by the juke box, seemed to be the meeting place for Dirk's crowd, for there were already several couples there. Lynn recognized among them a girl who had been at the movies with them. She and the boy she was with half-rose, beckoning to Dirk, and he turned toward them, drawing Lynn along with him.

"Hi there, Masters! We beat you!"

"You wouldn't have," Greta's date said loudly, "if Miss Chambers here hadn't thrown a fit on the way. It seems her father forbids her dates to drive at their own rate of speed. He makes them sign a statement that they will keep under thirty-five miles per hour at all times."

Everyone at the table roared.

Dirk hesitated a moment. Then he said in a rather flat voice, "That's all right. My dad's like that with Anne."

The laughter died a little. One of the boys said, "Oh, come off it, Masters. Your old man doesn't give a darn what you kids do."

"He does about Anne," Dirk said quietly. "Anne's a good girl, and don't let me hear you try to make her sound like anything else." He sat down at the edge of the booth, shoving the boy next to him over to make room, and motioned for Lynn to sit down beside him. "What'll you have?"

Lynn sat down, feeling out of place in her tan dress and pumps with heels. The other girls were dressed informally. One girl even had on slacks and a tight-fitting T-shirt.

"A Coke," Lynn said quietly to Dirk, hoping the others would not overhear her and find something else to laugh about.

"Just a Coke?"

"Yes, please."

Surprisingly, Dirk did not try to talk her into having anything else.

"O.K., a Coke it is."

He turned away from her to the group, who were laughing about something. One of the girls was telling a story in a high, shrill voice. The boys kept interrupting her to add comments of their own. Lynn thought the story might have been amusing if it had been about people she knew, but, as it was, she did not recognize any of the names or places mentioned, and she could not become interested. The comments from the boys did not make much sense to her, nor did the laughter when the story was over.

The drinks arrived, and she seized her Coke gratefully. With a glass to hold in her hand, she did not feel quite so uncomfortably out of things. To her relief, she saw that Dirk had ordered a Coke, too.

"What's the matter, Masters?" one of the boys asked. "Don't tell me you're on the wagon?"

"For tonight I am," Dirk answered quietly.

On the far side of the table, the girl with the shrill voice began another story.

There was a clock with flourescent hands over the bar. Sitting, facing it, Lynn thought she had never seen time move so slowly. The stories went on and on in a kind of monotonous hum, first one girl telling one and then another. The boys began to talk about automobiles. Lynn, who was never interested in automobiles, even when Paul was talking about them, transferred her attention to Greta, who was sitting across from her.

Greta caught her eye and giggled.

"Lynn Chambers remembered me," she said to the girl next to her. "Can you beat that? She remembered me."

The girl, who was older than Greta and Lynn, frowned in concentration.

"Who's Lynn Chambers?"

"That girl over there. The one with Dirky. She remembered me."

The older girl gave Lynn a half-apologetic look. "Don't

worry about her. She gets like this—sort of giggly and silly."

Lynn said, "That's all right."

She took another gulp of Coke, knowing that it was not all right. It was not all right at all. She could imagine the look on her parents' faces if they should walk into Charlie's at this moment and find her here with a group like this one. She glanced up at the clock. It was only eleven.

The crowd burst into loud laughter again at something one of the boys had said. Dirk was laughing with the rest.

Then suddenly somebody said, "Hi!"

Everyone turned. The laughter died a little.

Dirk turned with the rest of them, and he scowled slightly when he saw who was speaking.

"Oh, hi, Brad!"

The heavy-set boy who stood by the table could not have been more than a couple of years older than Dirk, but there was nothing young about him. His eyes were small and pale and set far apart and there was a look of hardness about him, even when he smiled.

He was smiling now.

He perched on the edge of the seat next to Lynn and leaned across to speak to Dirk. His breath was unpleasant, and Lynn, drawing back with a feeling of disgust, realized that he had been drinking heavily.

"Hi, Masters!" he said in a low, confidential voice. "Aren't you going to introduce me to your girl friend?"

"She's not—that is—" Dirk looked flustered. "This is Lynn Chambers—Brad Morgan."

Brad drew back a little so his face was next to Lynn's. "Hi, there, Lynn. You're a pretty cute little number. Want to dance?"

Lynn recoiled from his breath, trying desperately to think of something to say. She did not want to dance with this man. More than anything in the world she did not want to dance with him; the mere idea of it made her physically ill. But there was no polite way of getting out of it. The juke box was playing. People were dancing. They had just been formally introduced, and he had invited her to dance, and there seemed to be no polite way to refuse.

She glanced beseechingly at Dirk.

He reached over and put his hand on her arm.

"Not tonight Brad. Lynn and I have to push off. I promised her old man I'd get her home early."

"One little dance first?" Brad pleaded, leaning across Lynn again. "Don't be a spoil-sport, Masters. You wouldn't be having this evening if I hadn't lent you my car. You can return a favor with a favor, you know."

"Sorry," Dirk said shortly, "not tonight." He got to his feet. "Come on, Lynn."

Brad shook his head regretfully. "I should be mad at you, Masters, but I'm not. If I had a cute little number like that one, I'd hang on pretty tight myself. Some guys get all the breaks."

Lynn slid out of the booth quickly. Dirk took her arm and turned back to the group.

"So long, everybody! See you in the funny papers!"

"So long, Masters! Great seeing you, boy! Have fun!" Somebody said, "Good night, Lynn!" Brad said something else, calling it after them in a low voice, but Lynn did not understand him.

It was a relief to be out of the smoke-filled atmosphere and walking across the parking lot to the car. The air was clear and cold. There were stars.

Lynn shivered a little, wishing she had brought her coat She asked, "What did Brad mean about your borrowing his car? Is this his?"

Dirk nodded. He opened the door on the driver's side and Lynn got in, sliding across the seat to the opposite side.

"Why did he lend it to you? Is he a special friend of yours?"

"In a way." Dirk got in, shut the door and started the engine.

He backed the car out of the driveway and turned onto the main road. He drove slowly now and carefully.

"He's not like that all the time," he said. "Just when he's been drinking. Sometimes he's a neat guy. He's smart. Plenty smart in lots of ways."

"If he's so smart," Lynn said shortly, "why does he let himself get into the condition he was in tonight?"

"What's that got to do with being smart?" Dirk asked. "Everybody has too much to drink once in a while."

Lynn did not answer.

They drove the rest of the way in silence. When they pulled to a stop in front of her house, Lynn knew she should break the silence, but it was hard to think of something to say.

If it had been Paul, there would have been no problem. It was wonderfully easy to say good night to Paul, to say "Thank you for a lovely evening," and "I've had a wonderful time." But with Dirk it was difficult, because it had not been a lovely evening. It had been strained and uncomfortable and at times very unpleasant. And yet Dirk himself had seemed to be trying to give her a nice time. There had been no sarcasm, no smart-aleck remarks. He had treated her with respect in front of his friends, he had protected her from Brad's advances and when she was frightened at his driving, he had slowed down as she asked him.

She could feel him looking at her in the darkness. She forced herself to turn to meet his gaze.

"Dirk," she began, "thank you so much for a nice evening. It was a lot of fun; I had such a nice—"

"Did you?" His voice was low and gruff in the darkness, and there was a touch of warmth in it she had not heard before. "Did you really?"

"Yes," Lynn said, hoping she sounded convincing.

"Then what about kissing me good night?"

"Kissing you good night!" Lynn stared across at him, trying to see his face. Surely he was not serious. "But, Dirk, this is our first date. Besides, I don't just kiss everybody good night. Not just to say thank you for a nice evening! It has to be special, to mean something."

He was silent a moment and then he laughed, a funny, hoarse little laugh. When he spoke again, he sounded like the old Dirk.

"So you think you're too good, is that it? Too good to kiss Dirk Masters. This whole evening has been kind of a joke for you, hasn't it? Lynn Chambers, Princess of the Hill, going slumming."

"Why, no," Lynn exclaimed, "that's not true! It wasn't like that at all!"

And even as she said it, she felt a flush of guilt because it *had* been like that. Exactly as he said it.

"Oh, no?" Dirk slid forward across the seat until he was beside her. He put both hands on her shoulders and she could feel his warm breath against her face. "Well, you're not any better than I am. Not one bit better, and your wishy-washy Paul Kingsley isn't either. I bet you kiss him, don't you? No being coy or pulling away from *him*."

"That's different," Lynn whispered, wondering desperately how she could get away from Dirk and out of the car with his hands so strong on her shoulders. "Paul and I— well, Paul is special—he's—"

"Yeah. He's from the Hill."

And then he kissed her. It was a hard kiss, a determined kiss from a boy who had kissed girls before. There was nothing tender about it, nothing of the gentle awkwardness of Paul's first kiss the night he had asked her to go steady. Lynn had lifted her own face then and kissed him back, with a singing inside her and a glow of happiness that was almost too much to bear. There was no singing in her now, only a kind of terror, a longing to get away.

When Dirk finally released her, Lynn was trembling with anger.

"There," Dirk said, a note of satisfaction in his voice. "Did your Hill boy friend ever kiss you like that?"

"No," Lynn said, "and if he ever had, I would never have spoken to him again."

She opened the car door, slid through it and slammed it behind her. Without even a glance over her shoulder at the boy in the car, she ran up the porch steps and into the house.

5

When Lynn arrived at school the following Monday, the news was there before her. It was a muffled buzz all around her, a horrified whisper following her through the halls and into classrooms. "Lynn had a date with Dirk Masters! With *Dirk Masters!*"

Nancy was the first one to mention it. It was at the end of home room period, when they were free to talk for a few minutes before the bell. She turned around in her seat in front of Lynn's. She looked troubled.

"Is it true that you dated that Masters boy?"

Lynn was surprised. "Yes. How did you know?"

"Well, Joan's brother went to the movies Saturday night and said he saw you with him. That he had hold of your arm and that there was another couple with you, that terrible Greta something-or-other who sits in the back row of English class and some other boy. Lynn—" she hesitated, searching for the right words—"you don't have to do that, you know."

"To do what?"

'To date boys like that. I mean, it's tough about this debut business. We all wish your dad would let you take part in it and we feel mean not having you to our parties. We like you just as much as ever, Lynn. You don't have to prove anything—"

"I'm not proving anything," Lynn said irritably.

"Yes, you are. You must be. You'd never date a horrible boy like that if you weren't I—" She put an uncertain hand on her friend's arm— "I know it must be hard, being out of things and having all the Hill boys at the parties so there's nobody left to date, but just remember that Paul is going to be home soon. It will be Christmas vacation before you know it. You don't have to date boys like Dirk when you've got Paul."

"I know," Lynn said, with a sigh. "I know, Nan, and I guess you're right. I was just trying to prove something. Don't worry, I won't be going out with Dirk again."

"Well, good," Nancy said with satisfaction. She was silent a moment, and then she asked slowly, "What was it like?"

"What?"

"Dating Dirk. How did he act? Did he get fresh?"

"Yes," Lynn said, "sort of, at the last. He was pretty nice the rest of the time." She changed the subject with an effort. "How are the debutante parties coming? How was the dinner dance?"

"Oh, fine!" Nancy's face brightened. "It was more fun— you just can't imagine! You know what a lovely, big house Joan's folks have. We ate in the dining room, a formal affair, with everyone in dinner dress and candles on the table and the best silver and china, and they served—let's see—" She wrinkled her nose in an effort to remember. "Cornish hen, I think it was. And wild rice and peas cooked with mushrooms and fruit salad and a gorgeous ice cream thing for dessert. And after dinner we went into the living room and they had everything cleared and the room was decorated to represent the end of autumn—rust and gold and brown. And we danced—"

"Was there an orchestra?" Lynn asked, interested in spite of herself.

"No. Joan said they talked about it, but her father thought that would cost too much. As it was, the dinner must have cost a small fortune, with twenty girls and their dates."

"I should think so!" Lynn exclaimed. Suddenly a thought struck her. "Who did Brenda Peterson bring as a date?"

"I didn't know him. Some boy from out of town. A cousin, I think."

Lynn laughed heartlessly. "That sounds about right for Brenda. I guess she couldn't get any of the other boys to take her."

Nancy frowned. "That's not fair, Lynn. You know as well as I do that there aren't many surplus boys in the senior class—that is, suitable boys. Brenda hasn't been dating much, so naturally it's hard for her to latch on to one now. And everyone has to have an escort to these affairs, or they just don't work out." She gave Lynn an odd look. "You don't like Brenda at all, do you?"

"Do you?" Lynn countered. "She's always seemed such a blah little thing, I didn't think any of us were especially fond of her."

"That's true," Nancy admitted. "But now—I don't know—I'm beginning to think maybe I didn't give her a good chance before. Her mother lords it over her so much, it's hard to get to know what she's like underneath. These parties are the first chance I've had to really talk to her, and you know, she's not half bad. I think she could be a pretty swell girl if it weren't for her mother."

"Maybe," Lynn said reluctantly. "I don't know." She knew that her dislike for Brenda was unreasonable and had come into being only recently. For some reason, it seemed as though Brenda's entering the crowd and Lynn's leaving it had come simultaneously. It was as though she had been replaced by Brenda, as though, if Brenda were not there, she would be missed more by the others.

Which is ridiculous, Lynn told herself sternly. She saw that Nancy was on the verge of saying something else, and she was relieved when the bell rang and the chance for conversation ceased.

It was, however, not the end of the whispers about her date with Dirk. Several of the other girls mentioned it, playfully, but with a layer of seriousness underneath. Others seemed to let the conversation drag a little, as if they hoped she would fill it in with some details about her Saturday night. In the cafeteria, Rachel Goldman caught her eye and smiled, so did Clara Marivella. Anne's crowd too, it seemed, knew about the date, but they seemed to like Lynn better for it.

Dirk himself did not look at her at all. Lynn passed him once in the hall. She was sure he saw her; he really could not help it because he was walking directly toward her, but had turned his head slightly in passing, as though he were not aware she was there.

She was relieved in a way. She had certainly not been looking forward to talking to Dirk after their embarrassing parting. But she was peeved, too, in a way that she could not explain.

He could at least say hello, she thought irritably. After all, *he's* not the one who should be mad. If anybody's going to snub anybody, I'm the one who has the right to do it.

It was after she left the cafeteria and started into the main building for her usual study time that she saw Anne. She was standing alone by the door to the building, and when she saw Lynn coming, she stepped forward to meet her.

"Hi, Lynn! I've been waiting for you."

"Oh?" Lynn was surprised. She had somehow assumed that if Dirk was angry with her, Anne would be, too. Or perhaps it was the other way; she herself was angry with Dirk and, therefore, part of her feeling spilled over onto Anne. But now, looking at the girl, with her sweet mouth and honest brown eyes, Lynn felt any irritability slip quickly away.

"Hi! How are things going?"

"All right." Anne hesitated. "Could I talk to you for a few minutes?"

"Of course." Lynn followed the girl over to the bench they had sat on when they talked before. She sat down, wondering what it was Anne had to say.

Anne sat in silence a moment, as though she were having difficulty framing her words. Then, when she did speak, it was all in a rush.

"I know this isn't any of my business, and maybe you'll hate me for butting in like this, but I've got to talk to you about Dirk."

"About Dirk?"

"Yes. I don't know what happened on your date with him Saturday night. He didn't tell me, and I don't expect you to, but I know that when he came in that night he was more upset than I've ever seen him. He said it was all his fault, that he had done some crazy thing and he had disgusted you and made you furious. He didn't say what it was, just that it was foolish and that he was clumsy and stupid and would never be anything else, and then he stamped off to bed."

"I don't understand," Lynn said in bewilderment. "Why would he act like that? We did have a—a kind of misunderstanding—and I *was* mad, but I don't see why that should make any difference to Dirk. You know why he took me out; it was just sort of a thing he was forced into. It wasn't as though he really wanted me to like him or anything."

Anne said, "You really think that? That he doesn't care if you like him?"

"Of course," Lynn asserted. "Why, Dirk hasn't said one nice thing to me in as long as I've known him."

"Did you ever think," Anne asked softly, "that he might be afraid?"

"Afraid? Of what?"

"Afraid that maybe, if he did act as though he liked you, you would snub him? Or even worse, maybe laugh at him? Dirk can't bear to be laughed at."

"That's silly," Lynn said uncomfortably.

She thought, would I have snubbed him? Perhaps. Perhaps I would have. Lynn Chambers, secure in her crowd, Princess of the Hill, being sought after by somebody like Dirk Masters. Perhaps I would have done just that.

Anne continued talking in a low voice.

"You have to understand Dirk, Lynn. He's not like the boys your crowd usually goes around with. Dirk hasn't had an easy time. Our mother died when we were little; I was ten and Dirk was eleven. Dirk was Mother's pet and I was Dad's. I don't know why, but I picked up and went on all right. It was hard, but it wasn't impossible. But Dirk couldn't. He just sort of went wild. He started going around with a rough crowd of fellows and acting tough and hard, like they did. Then he met this Brad Morgan—"

"I know," Lynn put in. "I met him Saturday night."

"Well, then you saw what he's like. I don't know what Dirk sees in him." Anne hesitated and then corrected herself. "Yes, I guess I do know, at that Brad has a car, and Dirk is so car-crazy! Brad is always asking him to work on it with him. Dirk is really quite good at mechanical things like that, and I guess it flatters him to have Brad ask him to help. They have that car so souped up now that it goes like an airplane."

"I know." Lynn murmured.

"So Dirk works on the car, and in return Brad lends it to him sometimes. That's the basis for their friendship—that is, it used to be, but now I don't know. They're together so much! I worry about it Lynn. Brad's not good for Dirk. Last summer they got in trouble with the police, and that's not like Dirk. He's a nice boy, underneath. Sometimes he can be so sweet, so thoughtful as far as I am concerned. I just can't bear it to see him going wild the way he has been."

Lynn said, "What about your father? Can't he talk to him?"

"Poor Dad!" Anne shook her head. "Dad and Dirk never did get along too well, even when Mother was alive. Too much alike, I guess; they both have short tempers and get sulky when they're mad. When Mother died, Dad started working the night shift at the plant; it pays more, and we need the money. It works out all right but he's hardly ever at home when Dirk is, and when they are there together, they just argue about everything."

"That's awful," Lynn said sympathetically. "An awful situation, and especially for you. But why are you telling me about it? What can I do?"

"Dirk likes you," Anne said. "He always has, ever since the first time he saw you. If he's insulting and smart alecky with you, it's because he's afraid to show you how he feels. Don't ever let him find out that I told you this, but he said to me one time, 'I don't know why I bother to date the kind of gals Brad runs around with. I don't enjoy it. I guess it's because the one girl I ever really fell for would never look at me twice.' And I asked, 'Who is she?' And he kind of laughed, you know the hard way he laughs, but with sort of a broken sound to it too, and he said, 'You'll laugh at me, Anne, but I'm going to tell you. The girl who's about as far out of my reach as any I'll ever know. Who else but Lynn Chambers, the Princess of the Hill! Crazy, isn't it?' And then he laughed again, but it wasn't really laughing, and I could have cried for him."

"He said that!" Lynn exclaimed. "Oh, Anne, I didn't know! I never even guessed!"

She thought about Saturday night and her pretty little speech about how she just liked to be kissed by special people. It was true, of course, but it must have sounded to Dirk as though she just couldn't stand the thought of his touching her.

Her face burned at the memory.

"So whatever it was," Anne continued earnestly, "whatever he said or did—and knowing Dirk, I can imagine it was probably something pretty crude—please don't hold it against him. He needs somebody like you, Lynn. I'm just his sister. He loves me, of course, but a boy's sister never has much influence over him, especially when she is younger. *You* could."

"Do you think so?" Lynn was flattered in spite of herself. The thought of being an influence for good, of having the power to lead an erring boy into the light, was an exciting one. And Dirk, as his sister described him, sounded like a different person from the boy she had always thought of as Dirk Masters. Her mind flew back over the evening they had spent together—the little things—the way he had looked at her, the way he had taken her arm, the sound of his voice as he introduced her to his friends. She wished she could have seen his face when they sat in the parked car in front of her house. Perhaps, if she had, she would have seen something there that would have changed her answer when he asked her to kiss him.

"He probably won't feel that way now," she said slowly. "He was awfully angry when we wound up the evening. And today at school, he wouldn't even look at me when we passed in the hall."

Anne nodded. "He was probably too embarrassed to look at you. I think that whatever happened Saturday night, Dirk feels much worse about it than you do."

Lynn said, 'I'd like to help, but what can I do? I can't just walk up to him and say, "Let's have another date and try again.'"

"No," Anne agreed, "but you could get to know him

and be his friend. That is, if you are serious about wanting to."

"I am serious. But how?"

"Well," Anne answered hesitantly, "I—well—"

"What?"

"You could come home with me," Anne said quickly, avoiding Lynn's eyes. "To spend the night, I mean. You'd be there, and he'd be there, and it would kind of take care of itself. That is, if you do really want to."

Lynn hesitated. "Well—"

Spending the night at Anne's house was something that had never occurred to her as a possibility. Anne lived in a different world, a world with Rachel and Clara and the other girls she went around with. They probably all spent nights at each other's houses, just as Lynn spent nights with Nancy and Holly and Joan, but the idea of going to Anne Masters'—

She thought, what would Nancy say if I did? And Holly and Joan and the rest of them? Mother and Daddy wouldn't mind, I guess, but Dodie—Dodie would just pop!

The idea of Dodie's horror brought the touch of a smile to her lips.

"When would you like me to come?" she asked.

Anne raised her eyes and met Lynn's own with a look of gratitude.

"What about Friday? Would you like to come Friday?"

Lynn thought, Friday. That's the night of the next debutante party, the steak grill at the Taylors'.

The Taylors' house was only three lots away from the Chambers. From her room, she would hear the crowd laughing in the Taylors' backyard, the games, the singing, the music from Holly's hi-fi. She would sit there all evening, listening to the fun she could not join. It would be wonderful to go some place Friday night, some place entirely different from anywhere she had been before.

"Yes," she said, "Friday night would be fine. Thank you for asking me, Anne. I'd love to come Friday night."

6

The school bus dragged to a noisy stop, the door opened, and Lynn thankfully climbed off. She stood on the curb, clutching her overnight bag, while Anne clambered down the steps beside her. They stood together as the bus gave a weary roar and pulled away, to continue its tedious pace down the street.

Lynn glanced at her watch. "Four-thirty! My goodness, does it always take you an hour to get home?"

Anne nodded. "Sometimes more. The bus makes another trip before this one, and we have to wait for the second load. You're lucky living a couple of blocks away from the school. I feel as though I spend half my life on that creaky old school bus, either going or coming."

"What about Dirk?" Lynn asked. "Doesn't he ride it too?"

"Sometimes. Most of the time, though, he goes off after school with some of the fellows. Today, I saw Brad sitting in his car in the parking lot so I guess he was waiting to pick him up." Anne turned down the sidewalk. "Ours is the third house on the right. Can I help you carry your bag or anything?"

"No, thanks," Lynn answered. "I don't have anything in it except a toothbrush and pajamas."

She fell into step with Anne, glancing around at the neighborhood with veiled curiosity. She had often wondered what kind of district Dirk lived in. She had pictured a tenement type area, with bars scattered here and there and tough-looking boys in black leather jackets lounging around on street corners. That was what the poorer areas of town always looked like in movies. Now she was ashamed of herself in the light of what she saw.

True, the neighborhood she was now in was not to be compared with the Hill. It consisted of rows of very small houses, crammed closely together. Facing the street were rows of unpainted porches; and in tiny, unplanted front yards, dogs dug holes and old men sat and rocked and little children roughhoused. It was clearly a poorer section of town and quite different from the lovely residential areas, but there was nothing evil about it. In fact, it looked quite friendly.

Anne, seeing her interest, said, "There's Clara's house, over there, the one with the old lady sitting on the porch. That's her grandmother. She doesn't speak anything but Spanish, so nobody can talk to her, but she doesn't miss a thing that's going on along the street."

"Do any of the other kids from school live here?" Lynn asked.

"Well, I guess you know Ronnie Turner lives over there where the three little children are playing out front. I hope they didn't wear your sister out yesterday."

"What?" Lynn stared at her. "Wear who out?"

"Your sister. Her name's Dodie, isn't it?"

"Yes—Dodie," Lynn answered in bewilderment. "You mean Dodie was over here yesterday? For heaven's sake, why?"

"Goodness, I don't know," Anne said. "I didn't talk to her. I just noticed Ronnie arrive in that old rattle trap Ford he drives and let Dodie and the little kids off at the house and go off again. She took the kids inside. I thought you knew all about it."

Lynn could not believe her ears. "Are you sure it was Dodie?"

"Why, I think so." Anne dropped the subject as she turned up the steps of one of the houses. "And here we are—home. I know it's not anything compared to your house, but I've tried to make it nice. I do hope you like it."

She spoke with a touch of pride in her voice, and, as she entered, Lynn could see why. The small living room was so clean that the walls fairly sparkled. There were several cheap scatter rugs on the floor, but they were a soft moss green, and the ancient sofa and armchair were covered with the same soft color. There were bright print curtains hanging crisply at the window, looking as though they had only recently been starched and ironed, and on the walls were several gay street scenes, done in water colors and nicely framed in natural wood. There was a bowl of yellow straw flowers on a card table before the window.

"I don't have a sewing machine," Anne said, "but I made the curtains and slipcovers in Home Economics class. You should have seen me lugging those darned slipcovers back and forth on the school bus! I had to fit them almost every night, to make sure I was doing them right."

"You mean you made the sofa cover yourself?" Lynn exclaimed. "Why, Anne, you're a positive genius! I never knew anybody before who could make slipcovers. And those water colors are charming. Where did you ever find them?"

"I painted them," Anne told her simply.

"You painted them yourself!" Crossing the room, Lynn stood gazing at the pictures with a critical eye. "They're wonderful, so gay and full of life! I've always loved to draw, but I could never do anything like these. Why on earth aren't you in the Art Club?"

"I would be but—" Anne shook her head. "Oh, you know as well as I do that the Art Club belongs to the Hill crowd. It's more a social club than one devoted to art, isn't it?"

Lynn nodded. "I suppose it is, really," she admitted slowly. "I never thought of it that way before, but it *is* pretty much all the crowd from the Hill. That shouldn't make any difference, though, Anne. Not one of them can paint like this."

"It does make a difference, just the same," Anne said. "You know it does. I could go in there with my little paintings, and everybody would say, 'Aren't they clever?' and I'd still be just as much out of things as ever."

She spoke with no bitterness. Anne seemed to be a person incapable of bitterness. Shrugging her shoulders, she turned into the little hall. "Come on, I'll show you where we'll be sleeping tonight. You can unpack your things."

Lynn followed her through the hall into a tiny room. It was not really meant to be a bedroom—it was more like a pantry or a snug storeroom—but there was a bed in it, and Anne's deft touch had made it into a dainty little boudoir. The one small window was bordered with fluffy white material and the walls were painted pale blue. There was a checkered blue and white spread on the bed and a little gray chest of drawers with a mirror over it against the other wall.

"Not even room for a chair." Anne apologized, laughing, "but I guess we can sit on the bed. Dad and Dirk share the bedroom. They're never in it at the same time, though, because of Dad's working the night shift. Which reminds me, I'd better get his dinner ready. He goes to work at six."

She left Lynn to unpack her pajamas and other overnight things and lay them out on the bed.

Alone, Lynn glanced around the tiny room, wondering how Anne had managed to make such a charming place for herself out of what was no more than a cell. On the walls were more of the attractive water colors but these were softer scenes, little landscapes in blues and greens and golds. Lynn examined them more closely, her admiration growing.

I'd love to have some like these for my own room, she thought, but I don't know how to ask for them. Of course, I'd want to pay Anne for her work, and yet it would be awkward to offer her money.

She turned to follow her hostess out to the kitchen.

In the hall, she encountered Anne's father, emerging from the bedroom. He was a short, stocky man, with faded blue eyes and a heavy way of moving. Lynn quickly introduced herself, thinking that Anne and Dirk must both take their looks from their mother, for there was nothing of Mr. Masters in either of them.

Then, to her surprise, he smiled at her, and it was Anne's sweet smile that flashed from his weathered face.

"Lynn Chambers, huh? Well, I'm glad to meet you, Lynn. It's good to have Anne bringing her friends home with her. I wish that boy would do the same, but he seems to prefer to meet his pals on street corners."

He went on down the hallway and Lynn joined Anne in the kitchen. She stood as close to the wall as possible, trying not to get in the way as the other girl moved deftly about in the small space, preparing dinner.

"Is there anything I can do to help?"

"Yes," Anne said, "you can fix the salad. The greens are wrapped in a towel in the refrigerator."

Lynn opened the refrigerator door and took out the damp towel which held the salad ingredients, trying not to look surprised at how empty the refrigerator was. The Chambers' refrigerator was always overloaded with food for snacking—apples and plums and ice cream and Cokes and all manner of other things. Rosalie saw to that. The Masters' refrigerator contained the basic necessities—milk, eggs, margarine, some bacon and cheese—and a few covered jars.

Lynn shut the door and laid the salad greens on the counter.

While she cut up tomatoes and lettuce for a salad, she noticed how quickly and efficiently Anne went about her chores, putting peas on to cook, brewing tea, frying hamburgers. The meal seemed to fly together at her touch.

"Do you always do the cooking?" Lynn asked, greatly impressed.

"Almost always," Anne said, flipping the hamburgers onto the plate. "We eat sort of oddly because of Dad's working hours. He goes to work at six, so we have an early dinner. He gets off at two in the morning, so I leave a supper ready in the refrigerator for him to eat then. He's always asleep when Dirk and I get up, so we eat breakfast and leave the dishes for Dad to do when he wakes. He fixes himself a lunch, or breakfast, or whatever you want to call it, around ten. Then he has an afternoon job, working part time in Mr. Hendricks' Grocery Store."

'Two jobs!" Lynn exclaimed. "Why, he must be exhausted!"

"He is," Anne said, dropping her voice. "Sometimes I think maybe that's why he's so hard on Dirk. He's just so worn out, he can't relax and take things easy. And Dirk— well, Dirk could be making things easier for him if he wanted to. Other boys work in the afternoons, after school. Look at Ronnie Turner, for instance! But not Dirk; he's too busy with his own activities."

Lynn asked, "Will he be here for dinner?"

"I certainly hope so," Anne replied. "If not, this will be the third time this week that he's missed dinner, and Dad will be furious."

But Dirk did not show up. The meal was a hurried one, as Mr. Masters was running slightly behind schedule and had to be at his job in a short time. He bolted his food, scarcely stopping to chew it, got up quickly without excusing himself and snatched his jacket off the back of a nearby chair.

Now I know where Dirk gets his manners, or lack of them, Lynn thought with distaste. She could not remember ever seeing her father shovel food into his mouth or leave the table before her mother was finished, unless there was an emergency call from the hospital.

But then, she reminded herself sharply, Daddy's had advantages Mr. Masters hasn't enjoyed. Perhaps he was brought up this way and honestly doesn't know any better.

Her opinion of him softened as he stopped by her chair

and laid a hand briefly on her shoulder.

"I'm glad you came, Lynn. You and Anne have a good time together. Poor kid, she must get lonely in the evenings with nothing to do and no one to talk to." He turned to Anne.

" 'Night, baby. Thanks for dinner."

"Good night, Dad." Anne's face was tender as she rose to give her father a quick kiss. "I'll have something in the refrigerator for you when you come in."

"Fine!" Her father started for the door and then turned back. "When your brother gets in, you can tell him for me—

"Now, Dad," Anne broke in gently, "we don't know what delayed him. I'm sure he has a reason for not getting here in time to eat with us."

Her father did not bother to answer. He merely opened the front door and went out, shutting it a little too loudly behind him.

After helping Anne to do the dishes at the miniature kitchen sink, Lynn wondered what in the world they would find to do to pass the evening. It was only six-thirty and still light outside. There was no television set or record player, and she could not remember seeing even a radio. She glanced at Anne.

Anne caught the look and interpreted it correctly.

"There isn't much to do here in the evening. Usually, I study and read or paint for a while and go to bed early. Sometimes, when Dirk is here, we play cards together. Or I go over to Clara's, or walk downtown." Suddenly her face brightened. "Why don't we go to a movie?"

"Fine," Lynn said. "If we leave right away, we can make the early show."

They left the dishes stacked in the drying rack and caught the bus at the corner. When they reached the movie theater, she hesitated in the lobby, waiting for Anne to lead the way to where she wanted to sit. She was relieved to see that she did not choose the balcony. Though, there's no reason why she would, Lynn reminded herself. Anne may be Dirk's sister, but she certainly doesn't go around with the disgusting people he does.

The movie was a long one, and there were a lot of short subjects, so it was nine-thirty by the time they got out. They wandered through town, looking in lighted store windows, and stopped at a drugstore for a Coke before catching the bus for home. By the time they reached the Masters' house, another hour had passed, and it was almost half-past ten.

Dirk was sitting in the living room, eating a sandwich. His eyes widened when he saw Lynn.

"What the heck—"

Lynn smiled, enjoying his surprise. "Hello, Dirk; we missed you at dinner."

"Lynn is spending the night with me." Anne turned to him accusingly. "We *did* miss you at dinner, Dirk. Where were you?"

Dirk said, "Out."

"I know 'out.' Out where? With that Brad Morgan?"

"So, what if I was?" Dirk retorted defiantly. "I guess I'm old enough to pick my own friends." Then his voice softened before the concern in her face. "Don't worry about me so much, Annie. Be a good kid and run out to the kitchen and fry me a hamburger. I'm starved, and this peanut butter doesn't exactly hit the spot."

"All right, but you don't deserve it," Anne said.

She disappeared into the kitchen.

Lynn hesitated and then seated herself on the far end of the sofa. The silence was awkward.

She thought, I should say something—no, why should I be the one? Let Dirk speak first. I'm a guest in his house; let him be polite to me.

Dirk shifted uncomfortably.

Finally he said, "So you're spending the night with Anne? I didn't know you two were that close friends. I—I—" He fumbled for words. "I'm glad you did come."

It was the friendliest thing Dirk had ever said to her.

Lynn said, "I'm glad, too. I like your sister very much. I didn't realize before how talented she is. Why these water colors—" She gestured toward the walls. "They're just wonderful!"

Dirk brightened, his discomfort seeming to fall away.

"Aren't they good? She's never had any instruction, either. She just picks up a brush and goes to it, and those pictures come out." His face was gentle when he talked of his sister. "With all the work she does here, the housework and cooking and her schoolwork, you'd never think she'd have time to work on something like that. She's a great girl. She deserves a lot more than she's got."

"What do you mean?" Lynn asked softly.

"I mean at school mostly. Anne deserves to be in the clubs and on the student council and at all the parties—you know, one of the Crowd who run things. Just because she's so quiet and doesn't come from the Hill doesn't mean she doesn't have a lot on the ball!"

"Yes," agreed Lynn sincerely, "I realize that now. I never really knew Anne until recently. I guess I was too tied up with my own friends to try to get to know somebody else. But I do know her now, and I'm going to do everything I can to see she's included in everything that comes along."

Dirk was quiet a moment. Then he said, "Thanks." After a moment, he reached across and put his hand over hers. "About the other evening—I'm sorry."

He opened his mouth, as though he were going to say more, and then he closed it again. Lynn felt his hand tremble over hers. She turned toward him and found him looking at her. There was nothing defiant in his eyes now, nothing mocking. She felt strangely confused by the intensity of his gaze.

"That's all right, Dirk," she said, surprised by the tremor in her voice. "I—I guess— Let's forget about it, shall we?"

He nodded without speaking.

They sat there in companionable silence, listening to the clatter of dishes from the kitchen. The little room was warm and cozy in the light from the lamp on the table.

Lynn thought, I've never seen Dirk like this, just relaxed and comfortable and happy. He's always fighting something when I see him at school, trying to get the best of somebody, to show the world that he doesn't care. He's much nicer like this. And much more attractive.

Later that night, when she lay beside Anne in the narrow bed, Lynn thought about Dirk again.

He *is* a nice boy, she decided. Underneath all that hardness, there's somebody worth knowing. Maybe he's confused and doesn't know which direction to take, but that's because he doesn't have a mother to help him. People react in different ways to loneliness. Somebody like Anne matures with it and learns to take over and bear up and live things through. But somebody like Dirk, somebody not quite as strong as Anne, can go to pieces.

She thought, he needs somebody! He really does!

It was a strange thought, Dirk needing somebody.

Lying there in the cramped bed, listening to Anne's quiet breathing beside her, it was exciting to think of leading a wandering boy back onto the right path—exciting and inspiring and a tremendous challenge.

But as sleep came closer and the day's events slipped further away, it was not Dirk's handsome face that stayed in her mind. It was another face, one with a square, determined chin and an easy smile and honest blue eyes. Drowsily, Lynn raised her hand, felt for the chain around her throat and slid her fingers down it until they touched the ring.

"You're my girl," Paul had said. "We've got something between us worth hanging on to."

Oh, Paul, Lynn whispered into the pillow, I miss you! I miss you! I miss you so much!

And the ache of loneliness inside her was something that nobody else, no matter how much he needed her, could take away.

7

When Lynn stepped into her house late the next morning, she felt as though she were returning from a long journey. The city bus dropped her off at the corner of the Hill and River Road and she walked the rest of the way up the Hill toward the house, carrying her small overnight bag.

The air was crisp and cold, colder than the brisk chill of autumn, more like the beginning breath of winter before the first snow. Sunlight fell, bright and golden, through the half-naked branches of the maples which lined the walk, and the spacious lawns of the houses along the Hill were browning with the touch of frost.

As she passed the Taylor house, she wondered how the barbecue had gone the night before. She could imagine how it had been, the smell of charcoal rising from the huge outdoor grill in the back yard, the hi-fi playing, the laughter and talking during dinner, the singing afterward and perhaps dancing in the living room, if the night grew too cold for people to want to stay outside.

I'm glad I wasn't here, Lynn thought. If I had been, I would have felt so left out. I'm glad I went to Anne's. I feel as though I know her better now—and Dirk, too.

She turned in her own driveway and crossed the lawn to the house. She was conscious for the first time of what a large house it was, how wide the front porch, how spacious the front hall, how roomy and well-furnished the living room.

"Mother!"

"Hi, honey!" Her mother's voice came from the kitchen. Lynn had forgotten that Saturday afternoons were Rosalie's time off. She swung through the open door to find her mother elbow-deep in flour.

"Baking?"

"Yes." Mrs. Chambers glanced up self-consciously. "Come in, but don't you dare laugh. I know I don't do these things as well as Rosalie does, but I certainly love to try."

Lynn perched on the kitchen stool at one end of the table, shaking her head in astonishment at the mounds of ingredients that were piled in various places around the table surface, waiting to be poured into the gigantic mixing bowl. She could hardly keep back a smile when she remembered Anne's efficient cooking techniques.

"You love to cook, don't you, Mother? You can hardly wait for Rosalie's day off, so you can get in here and mess around."

"Mess around!" Mrs. Chambers exclaimed in mock horror. "Why, I'll have you know I'm making the best apple upside-down cake that has ever been eaten in this house!" Then she smiled. "Truly, I do love to mess around when it's something special, a real project of some kind. I don't like the regular everyday meals and I'm happy Rosalie does them for me; but then I'm delighted when the weekend comes and I can experiment with something interesting." She lifted one of the piles of flour and poured it into the bowl. "Did you have a good time at the Masters'?"

"Yes," Lynn answered, "Anne really is a good house-keeper. You know, she has been taking care of all the house-work and cooking and everything, all by herself, since her mother died."

"That's a big load for a girl her age," Mrs. Chambers said gravely. "What is Mr. Masters like?"

"He seems very nice," Lynn said, "although he works in the evenings, so I didn't have much chance to get to know him. Anne and I went to a movie. I seem to be seeing quite a lot of movies lately, don't I?"

Mrs. Chambers nodded. "Yes, you did just see one with Dirk, didn't you?" She began to rub flour on her hands. "Lynn, I've been wanting to talk to you about Dirk. Some of the ladies at the auxiliary meetings—well, their daughters have mentioned him at home— They all seem to think he isn't the kind of boy you should be dating."

Lynn straightened up. "Why?"

"Well, they say he has been in trouble with the police, that he runs around with an older crowd, that he smokes and drinks—all in all, that he just isn't desirable company for a girl like you. I wouldn't discuss it with them because I didn't really know anything about it. I just took it for grant-ed that he must be a nice boy or you would not be dating him."

"He is nice," Lynn said flatly. "I didn't think so at first but now I do. He's just sort of—well, mixed up. He needs somebody to help him."

Mrs. Chambers raised her eyes and gave her daughter a long look. "And that somebody is you?"

Lynn flushed. "Well, why not? He seems to like and respect me. Why not try to help him?"

"That's a good question," her mother answered quietly. "I don't know if there is as good an answer. I can only tell you what I have observed myself, through a few more years of living than you have had." She paused. "It's good to be friends with people and to like them and want to help them, but no boy is going to be helped by a girl unless he is willing to help himself first. And no girl is going to help a boy by leaning down to him. She can help him only by standing up tall and inspiring him to rise up to her."

"What do you mean?" Lynn asked uncomfortably, recalling with a flood of guilt the date with Dirk, the fast driving, the evening at Charlie's.

She thought, she can't know. There's no possible way for her to know about that.

Still, she was relieved when her mother said, "I'm not referring to anything special, dear; I'm just stating a generalization. And I'm wondering if maybe it would be better for you not to go out with this boy. There is no sense in asking for trouble when there is no need to."

"Not go out with this boy!" Lynn repeated, with a touch of bitterness in her voice. "Honestly, Mother, what do you and Daddy want me to do with myself during my senior year? You've forbidden me to be a debutante, which automatically cuts me out of dates with all the Hill boys. Now you're forbidding me to date boys who aren't Hill boys—"

"Lynn, that's not so!" her mother exclaimed. "I'm not thinking in terms of Hill boys and other boys. There are plenty of nice boys who don't come from the Hill. But this Dirk just sounds like a bad apple, a weakling and a troublemaker. I would think that of him wherever he came from. Daddy and I want you to be democratic in your friendships, but that doesn't mean you have to go out and deliberately pick out the worst possible boy you can find—"

"Oh, Mother!" Lynn swung herself off the stool. "For goodness' sakes, you're making so much more of everything than there is! But let's not argue about it. Goodness, it's already the end of November! Just two more weeks and Paul will be home, and then there won't be anything to worry about. I take it, you don't object to my dating Paul?"

"Oh, don't be silly!" Her mother sighed. "You know we don't object to Paul. Or to any other nice boy."

Lynn said, "I'm going up to my room and unpack my pajamas and things. Hope that cake's ready in time for lunch, I'm starved."

She went up the stairs, encountering Dodie in the hall. Her sister had her hair done up in pincurls, under a bright colored bandana.

She said, "Hi! You back?"

"Yes. What are you doing with your hair up at this hour?"

"Rolled it last night and it didn't take right so I'm doing it again. Can I use your hair dryer?"

"Sure, I guess so. But don't drop it." Lynn went into her room and got the little electric dryer out of her closet. "Hey, wait a minute before you go; I want to ask you something. Were you over at the Turners' house the other day?"

Dodie gave her a sharp glance. "Why?"

"Anne said she saw you there. I didn't think she could be right, but I thought I'd ask you, anyway."

"Yes," Dodie said surprisingly, "I was there. Mrs. Turner was at the hospital, visiting with the little girl, and Ronnie had to work, so I said I'd keep an eye on the boys."

Lynn's eyes opened wider. "How on earth did that happen? I mean, how did Ronnie come to ask you?"

"He didn't." Dodie answered briefly. "I asked him." She started toward the door and then she turned back, as though she felt she should add something to her explanation. "I went in the drugstore with the gang after school and Ronnie was trying to serve everybody and keep an eye on the three little kids at the same time. He had them in a back booth, and the little one was howling, and the other two were climbing on the table. Ronnie looked like he was about to have a breakdown, watching them and working at the same time, so I told him I'd babysit for a while."

Lynn stared at her younger sister in bewilderment. Was this Dodie—Dodie, who had never condescended to babysit in her entire life!

"I thought you hated babysitting."

"I do," Dodie said.

"Then, why—"

"Oh, I don't know!" Dodie exclaimed impatiently. "He just looked like he needed help. Now, can I get out of this third degree and go dry my hair?"

"Sure. Sorry to waste your valuable time," Lynn sat down on the bed.

Dodie, she thought, Dodie—I don't know you at all! You are my own sister, and you're more of a stranger to me than any girl I know. Why, I even know Anne better than I do you!

With the thought of Anne, she let her mind drift back to the night before, to the crowded little house and the tiny bedroom and the unfamiliar sounds that filled the night. She had not slept well. To begin with, she had never shared a bed with anyone before and she had been afraid to turn or even to move, for fear she would awaken Anne, who slept so soundly beside her. Then, there were no lawns to separate the house from the street. It seemed to Lynn as though the bedroom was set right in the middle of a highway, for each car that passed sent its headlights brightly through the window, and the night sounds—people passing along the sidewalk, the screech of brakes at the comer, the rumble of a train somewhere much too close, seemed to be rocking the house with their noise.

Besides that the house itself was so small that every sound leaped through the thin walls. She was very conscious of Dirk in the next room. She could hear him rise and go into the bathroom for a glass of water; she could hear the sound as he brushed his teeth and the gurgle of water as he took his shower and even the click of the bedside light as he settled himself to sleep. Then, at two in the morning, when Mr. Masters returned home, she woke immediately at the sound of his footsteps in the living room. She lay awake, listening to the refrigerator door open and close as he took out the supper Anne had left for him, the sound of a chair being drawn up to a table, and later, water running in the kitchen sink as he rinsed the dishes and then went into the bedroom.

I never realized, Lynn thought, how well built our house is. There are so many things I never realized.

She relaxed on the bed and shut her eyes. After her restless night, the bed seemed heavenly—wide and soft and inviting.

How long she slept, Lynn did not know, but when she awakened, it was to the sound of the telephone ringing in the hall. She sat up as she heard Dodie calling her name.

"Coming!"

She swung her legs over the side of the bed and went out into the hall, still hazy with sleep. She picked up the receiver. "Hello?"

"Hi, Lynn." It was Nancy. "I just wanted to tell you how much we missed you last night. Holly's party was just colossal, but we all wished so much that you could be there."

"Thanks," Lynn said, sitting down on the stool by the telephone table. "I had a pretty nice evening myself. I spent the night with Anne."

"Anne Masters?" Nancy did not sound as surprised as Lynn had thought she would. "She's a pretty nice girl, isn't she? I always thought I'd like to know her better but you just get going with one crowd—"

"I know," Lynn said. "She's awfully talented at painting. You should see her water colors! I'm going to see about voting her into the Art Club."

"I thought you'd dropped out of the Art Club."

"Well, maybe I'll drop back in again. I'm not sure," Lynn said. "What do you hear from that brother of mine?"

"I got a grand long letter just today. He says he and Paul can hardly wait to get home. He's all excited about taking me to the Christmas parties. Just think, one every night and real orchestras for some of them, and one will be a dinner party at the Yacht Club, and Mrs. Peterson is having a treasure hunt—" She stopped short. "Oh, Lynn, I'm sorry! Here I rattle on and on, and I keep forgetting you're not going to them. Please forgive me. I'm just as rude as I can be. It's just—well, you and I have always done the same things. It's so hard to remember—"

"Don't worry about it," Lynn said. "I really don't care. Paul will be home, and that's all tbat matters to me. We'll have a grand time together, even if we don't do anything but sit home and watch television every evening."

"Of course, you will. Well, I've got to go now; lunch is ready. I just wanted to check in and say 'hi.' I feel as though I never see you any more, Lynn. I miss you."

"You're just busy," Lynn said. "I understand that. And I'm busy too, only with different things. We'll make a real business of getting together soon. Why don't you come over and spend the night?"

"I will. Or you come here," Nancy said warmly. "Well, I'll see you."

"I'll see you," Lynn echoed. She drew a deep breath and replaced the receiver on the hook.

The smell of her mother's apple upside down cake floated up the stairs, and Lynn realized again that she was hungry—

More than just hungry, she was starving. She hurried into the bathroom and washed her hands and face, then went down the stairs.

Dodie and her mother were already eating lunch in the kitchen. Mrs. Chambers looked up and smiled.

"Sit down and have a sandwich. We're eating the lazy way. There doesn't seem to be much sense to carrying everything into the dining room when Rosalie isn't here to clear it away."

"No sense at all," Lynn agreed, going to the bread box and glancing around for something for a sandwich. She saw a jar of ham salad open on the counter, where Dodie had evidently placed it after making her own lunch. "Here, this looks good."

As she came around to seat herself at the kitchen table, Lynn stooped to drop a pensive kiss on her mother's forehead. "Sorry I was such a bear when we were talking before. I know you were just trying to give me some good advice."

Her mother nodded. "Maybe I shouldn't have. Maybe these things are the kind you have to work out for yourself. We won't talk about it any more, all right?"

"All right," Lynn said gratefully.

Dodie had been listening to this exchange with interest "What aren't you going to talk about any more?"

"None of your business," Lynn said, seating herself at the table and reaching across her sister for a napkin.

"Now, girls—" Mrs. Chambers' voice paused at the sound of the telephone.

Dodie was on her feet in an instant. "I'll get it."

She disappeared into the living room and Mrs. Chambers glanced at Lynn in a puzzled way. "Dodie's been jumping so at the telephone lately, I'm inclined to believe she's really interested in some boy. She hasn't mentioned anybody, though."

"If I didn't know Dodie," Lynn said, "I'd think it might be the Turner boy. But I can't imagine Dodie falling for somebody who wasn't part of her gang. Can you?"

"I don't know—" Mrs. Chambers said.

Dodie came back into the room.

"That was Janie. She has some more news about the debutantes!"

Lynn could not resist asking, "What is it?"

"Well," Dodie said, "there's evidently been some criticism from some people in town about so much money being spent on anything as 'useless' as debuts, when there are more valuable things that could be done with it. And Mrs. Peterson can't stand being criticized, so now she's worked out a civic project for the debutantes."

"A civic project!" Mrs. Chambers smiled in spite of herself. "That woman—it takes a lot to beat her! Well, what is her idea now?"

"A fashion show," reported Dodie. "It will be the last evening of the Christmas holidays, and everyone in town will be invited, and the debutantes themselves will model clothes from all the best shops. And then, as a grand finale, they are all going to come out modeling the gowns they are going to wear at their debut in the spring."

"That should bring quite a turnout," Mrs. Chambers admitted. "But what does it have to do with a civic project?"

"All the money they take in," Dodie said, "will be donated to the Rivertown Memorial Hospital."

8

"Pot roast and noodles and green peas and apple pie. Does that sound like the right welcome home meal?" Mrs. Chambers sat with her pen poised over her marketing list, her eyes shining. "Can you think of anything else, Lynn?"

"Peppermint ice cream," Lynn suggested. "You know how Ernie loves peppermint ice cream." She smiled at her mother. "You're not *very* excited, are you, Mother? Why, you'd think Ern had been gone three years instead of three months!"

"Well, it seems like three years to me," Mrs. Chambers said. "After all, it's the first time any of you children have been away from home—really away, I mean—and a boy's first college vacation is a very important thing. I want every-thing to be exactly right, so he'll know how glad we are he's home."

"Oh, he'll know," Lynn said fondly, watching her mother's eager face. "Just one look at you, and he'll know; don't worry about that. And when he sees the pot roast and noodles —ugh, what a combination—and the pie—"

"And the peppermint ice cream," added Mrs. Chambers, quickly jotting the item down on the list. She laughed. "I know I'm silly, but I'll be so glad to see him!"

"You're not being silly," Lynn said gently. "We'll all be glad to see Ernie. And Paul."

In her own mind, the fact that Paul was coming, that he was driving home in the same car as Ernie and would be here at last for the holidays, was even more exciting than the return of her brother. She loved Ernie, of course, and it would be grand to have him thumping around the house again, but Paul—

She took a long breath and let it out slowly, and automatically her fingers flew to the chain around her neck. Had it only been three months since Paul had given it to her? She had teased her mother about feeling as though Ernie had been gone three years instead, but now, somehow, it did not seem so funny. It did seem like years since she had seen Paul. It seemed longer, perhaps, because the three mtonths had been such odd ones, filled with the loneliness of not being one of the crowd any longer and the beginnings of new friendships with people she had not known before. There was so much to tell Paul, so much that could not be put into letters.

She had tried.

"Now that I'm definitely not going to be a debutante," she had written, "I seem to have nothing in common with the Hill crowd any longer. I can't go to any of their parties, and the parties are all they talk about these days. I can't even take part in their charity fashion show. I still go around with Nancy some, but that's more because I'm Ernie's sister than anything else. When we're together, we can always talk about Ernie. It's going to seem so funny not doubling with them this Christmas, isn't it—imagine just sitting home while everyone else goes to the big holiday parties?"

She had waited nervously for his answering letter, hoping desperately that the thought of missing all the holiday fun would not be too disappointing to him. When it arrived, she drew a breath of relief. It was a long, rambling letter, full of the usual college news, and at the very end, almost as an afterthought, he had written, "So we miss a few parties? So what?" And that had been the end of it.

And now Paul was coming home. Missing the parties did not seem important to Lynn any more either. Paul was coming home. A day had never crawled by with such maddening slowness as the day before he was to arrive.

"Don't you think we should wait up for them?" she asked that night.

Her mother laughed. "My goodness, Lynn, they were leaving after classes this afternoon. That means, if they stop for dinner some place, they couldn't possibly be home before four o'clock in the morning. Ernie will probably just come clomping in and fall into bed, and Paul isn't going to feel like doing any visiting either. He'll be headed for his own home."

"I suppose so," Lynn said.

Nevertheless, she slept lightly, half listening for the sound of the car in the driveway. When it came, she awoke. She lay very still in bed, listening to the various noises of arrival —the slam of a car door, the muffled sound of boys' voices, trying to be quiet, the thump of a suitcase being dragged up the porch steps and the rattle of the front door.

Unable to stand it any longer, Lyon hopped out of bed, pulled on her heavy quilted housecoat and slipped down the stairs.

Ernie was just coming in the front door. His eyes were

red and bleary, as though he had been asleep in the back seat of the car, but he looked up and grinned at her.

"Hi, Sis! Where is everybody?"

"Asleep in bed, idiot," Lynn retorted, surprised by the sudden flood of affection she felt at the sight of her brother. "After all, it's almost morning."

"Don't I know it!" Ernie exclaimed, dumping his suitcase unceremoniously onto the floor. "I've been asleep for the last hundred miles and Paul's been driving. Messy driving too, wasn't it, fellow? It's started to snow."

"It sure has. It looks as though we're going to have a white Christmas." Paul stood in the doorway. At the sound of his voice, Lynn felt a tightening in her chest. She wanted to look at him, but suddenly, amazingly, she was afraid.

She kept her eyes on Ernie. "Do you boys want something to eat?"

"I do," Ernie declared. "Come on, Paul, let's raid the icebox."

"Not me," Paul said. "I've got to be getting home. Mom's the 'waiting up' kind."

"Well, give me a call tomorrow then." Ernie said, disappearing in the direction of the kitchen. "Not too early, though. I'm going to sleep till noon."

"O.K."

The kitchen door swung closed behind him.

There was no excuse for not looking at Paul now. Lynn raised her eyes tentatively.

She thought, please! Please don't have changed!

He was standing by the door, one hand awkwardly on the knob, his face ruddy with the cold.

Lynn thought, he's so tall! I never realized before how

tall he is. And so much older looking, so kind of sophisticated! What will he think of me now? Will I seem terribly young to him? He's used to sophisticated college girls. Maybe there's even a special girl—one he didn't want to write me about. Maybe—

She was very conscious of her uncombed hair, of the lack of make-up, of the old blue housecoat. She said, "Hi."

"Hi!"

Paul took his hand off the doorknob, and Lynn crossed the room to him, feeling the strangeness inside her.

Please, like me she thought. Oh, please, don't have changed! I couldn't bear it if you had changed!

Paul put his hand gently beneath her chin and tilted her head up so he could look her full in the face. He let his fingers run down the side of her neck . . . and then he grinned, and with the grin, the old Paul was back again, just as though he had never been away. And suddenly Lynn was not afraid any longer.

"You're still wearing it. I was afraid maybe you weren't I mean—well, darn it, I don't know why I was so worried. It was crazy—"

"I know," Lynn said, smiling back at him, "but I was, too—worried, I mean. That maybe things wouldn't be the way they were. That you would have met somebody else."

"For gosh sakes," Paul said gruffly, "do you think I hand out rings to every girl who comes along? Of course, there's nobody else. But what about you—"

"Nobody else," Lynn said happily. "For gosh sakes," she said, imitating his tone of voice, "do you think I wear every ring that comes along?"

"You better not!" he asserted. He kissed her then.

Gently, the way he always kissed her.

And Lynn, standing on her tiptoes, thought he's so tall! I'd forgotten how tall!

He tightened his arms around her. "Still my girl? I've missed you like the very dickens." He released her. "Look what I've done, I've gotten you all wet. I didn't know I had so much snow on this jacket."

"It's no permanent damage," Lynn said happily. "Can't you sit down for a few minutes? There's so much to talk about I want to hear all about college, and there are so many things I couldn't get into my letters."

"I'd like to," Paul said, "but I've got to get home. Mom will be awake, and if I don't get in soon, she'll think we had a wreck some place. Mom is like that. Besides, your folks wouldn't be too keen on it either, at this hour."

"No," Lynn admitted. "Well, we've got two whole weeks, anyway."

"Sure, plenty of time." He gave her hand a quick squeeze. "I'll call you tomorrow. O.K.?"

"O.K.," Lynn said. "Good night"

She stood for a few moments after he had shut the door, listening to his footsteps on the porch, the opening and closing of the car door, the start of the engine. Then she let out her breath in a long sigh.

Paul is home!

It was a singing deep within her.

Paul is home, and it's just the way it always was!

This time, when she went to sleep, she slept hard. It was full-fledged morning, when she awoke again.

She knew when she first opened her eyes that there was something different about the day. The light in her room was different and there was a strange, glaring quality to it that made her squint her eyes. Sunlight flooded through the windows with a stark, blinding whiteness. It did not take the memory of Paul's words the night before to tell her that it had snowed.

A glance out the window confirmed the fact. The dead, dried lawn was covered with a blanket of whiteness. Even the branches of the trees outside the window were thinly coated with white, and she could see Holly's younger brother was already outside in his snowsuit, trying to scrape together the beginning of a snowman, over in the Taylors' back yard.

Lynn fought back an impulse to join him. So short a time ago it seemed, she and Ernie had been out on the lawn with the first snowfall, eagerly dragging along their sleds and throwing snowballs. Dodie had sometimes come too, but usually they were too busy for her. Dodie was always having to be taken care of because she was so small for her age.

So short a time ago. But now Lynn was a senior in high school and Ernie a college freshman, and it was Holly's little brother who ran shouting in the yard. Lynn took a deep breath, with an odd feeling of having lost something, and drew the window closed.

Downstairs, her mother and Dodie were eating breakfast. Lynn arrived just as Rosalie brought in a sizzling platter of eggs and bacon. She slipped into her place at the table and smiled across at her mother.

"I see old Ernie didn't make it downstairs yet. What do you bet he sleeps until lunch time?"

Her mother smiled back. "I'm placing no bets. I heard

him banging around in the kitchen about four this morning, so I came down and fed him. I've seen him, at least and now I don't care how long he sleeps. The longer the better."

Dr. Chambers came in just as the rest of them were finishing breakfast.

"What's the idea," he demanded irritably, "letting me oversleep on a weekday morning? You know I'm supposed to be at the hospital by eight o'clock."

"I know," his wife sighed. "It's just that you were out so long last night on that emergency call, I thought you might pick up just a little extra sleep."

Dodie glanced up. "What kind of emergency, Dad?"

"Automobile wreck," Dr. Chambers told her. "Some crazy kids, out drinking—snow on the road—it all adds up to a nasty experience. Nobody was killed, but one of the girls got cut up a little and had to be taken to the hospital. Burly, I think her name was. She's just about your age, Lynn."

"Burly?" Lynn nodded. "Greta Burly. Yes, I know her." She hesitated, half afraid to ask. "The boy—the one who was driving—"

"Never saw him before," her father said. "An older fellow. Should have known better. These crazy kids."

He stirred sugar into a cup of coffee, gulped it down and started for the door.

"No time for eating now. I'll see you tonight."

"Nathan Chambers, you send out for something when you get to the office!" his wife called after him, rising in her chair. "For a doctor, you take the worst care of yourself —"
She shook her head helplessly at the sound of the closing door cutting off her protest. "Your father works too hard,

girls. I don't know what in the world to do about him."

Lynn nodded, hardly listening. Her father's words swam in her head—"crazy kids, out drinking, driving—cut up a little, hospital—" She thought, thank goodness it wasn't Dirk! But it could have been. Dirk's just as crazy as the rest of them, and it could have been. And the girl—it might not have been Greta! If it had happened the other night, it might have been me!

The rest of her breakfast was tasteless in her mouth. It was not until her mother asked, "Do you have a date with Paul tonight?" that she was able to get her mind focused on pleasanter things.

"Yes," she said. "That is, we don't exactly have any plans, but I'm sure we will go out some place. He's going to phone me." She hesitated, an idea taking form in her mind. "I know! Why don't I have a party? Just a spur of the moment kind of get-together for all the kids; a sort of welcome home party for Paul and Ernie. It could be a plaid shirts-and-bluejeans affair, and we could play records and gab and I could ask the girls to come a little early and help make cocoa—"

"Sorry to nip your plan in the bud," Dodie inserted dryly, "but isn't there a debutante party tonight? Seems to me I heard some of the kids talking about it. The first big Christmas party, I think it is, a formal dance with orchestra and all."

"Oh, that's right" Lynn said. "I forgot; it's going to be at the Country Club." She frowned. "Then that cancels out any plans for a welcome home party, unless we had it tomorrow night instead."

"There's bound to be something tomorrow night,"

Dodie said. "The way I understood it there's going to be something planned for every single night during the vacation, except Christmas Eve."

Lynn sighed. "Well, that's that then. I guess Ernie will be going to all of them too, with Nancy. That kind of leaves Paul and me out in the cold."

"Don't feel too badly about it dear," her mother said gently. "I'm sure you and Paul will find lots of nice things to do."

"Oh, of course," Lynn said quickly. "It really doesn't matter. Just having Paul home is what counts, even if we don't do anything the whole vacation but sit right here in this living room, watching television. But we will probably be doing something more exciting than that tonight, on Paul's first night home!"

She got up from the table. "Excuse me, please. I want to make sure that I've got a dress pressed."

All morning, Lynn kept one ear open for the sound of the telephone. She pressed her dress and straightened her room and put her hair in pincurls and manicured her nails—all things she disliked doing, but things that really should be done, and at least they filled the morning.

She was not too surprised when the telephone call did not come by noon, for Ernie was still asleep and she assumed Paul was, too. By early afternoon, however, when Ernie had emerged from his bedroom, dressed, eaten and taken off for Nancy's house, she began to grow more impatient.

By the middle of the afternoon, she was really irritated. "After all," she said to her mother, "he must realize I'll want to know what the plans are. I want to know what time he's coming and what to wear and whether or not to eat dinner first. We didn't decide a thing last night."

"Don't be so impatient, dear," her mother said. "Paul isn't a thoughtless boy; you know that. He'll call just as soon as he has a chance. Maybe his mother had something she wanted him to do with her this afternoon, and he just couldn't get away to phone you."

"Anybody can find a way to get to a telephone," Lynn said, "if they really want to."

By the time the phone finally rang, at a quarter past five, she was thoroughly angry.

"Lynn?" Paul's voice was surprisingly deep over the telephone. "I'm sorry I couldn't call sooner."

"I thought you'd forgotten me entirely," Lynn said, her irritation showing in her voice. "I don't even know what the plans are for tonight. When are you coming by?"

"Well, that's what I wanted to tell you," Paul said awkwardly. "I won't be coming. Not tonight. I'm sorry, Lynn, because I certainly want to, but I've been sucked into going to this formal dance and there's no way I can get out of it."

"A formal dance!" Lynn exclaimed. "But Paul, how can you? The formal dance is the one at the Country Club, and that's only for the debutantes and their dates."

"I know," Paul said. "I'm taking Brenda Peterson."

"Brenda Peterson!" Lynn could hardly force out the words.

"Now, hold on a minute," Paul said, "let me explain. I was all set to call you this afternoon—I thought maybe we'd take in a movie or something tonight—when the phone rang. It was Mrs. Peterson, all upset. It seems she started this debutante thing in the first place, and they've had a lot of lesser parties which have worked out pretty well, but tonight's the night of the first real formal dance and Brenda doesn't have a date. Here Mrs. Peterson started it all, and now the formal comes and Brenda's stuck without an escort. She said the kid was all broken up and thought she'd be the laughing stock of the school if she didn't turn up at the party. Oh, you know how it is. So, she asked me if I'd take her."

"And you said "yes'?"

"Of course, I said 'yes,' " Paul answered. "What else could I say?"

"You could say 'no,' " Lynn told him, disappointment rising up sharply within her. "You could say, 'I'm sorry, but I already have a date. I go steady with Lynn Chambers, you know.' Why did Mrs. Peterson call you in the first place?"

"Oh, her husband was a friend of Dad's," Paul said. "They used to play golf together on Sundays. I guess she feels kind of a family attachment from that. Honestly, Lynn, I feel rotten about this, but I don't know how else I could have handled it. I could have said 'no' I guess, but I felt so sorry for the poor Peterson kid, stuck all by herself at home—"

"What about the poor Chambers kid, stuck all by herself at home?" Lynn said sharply. "I guess she doesn't matter?"

"Oh, come off it," Paul was beginning to sound irritated himself. "That's a different situation entirely. You're not a debutante. You don't have to turn out for these things. Nobody's going to laugh at *you* for missing one, but for a kid like Brenda—well, she's so darned unattractive to start with—if she couldn't even get somebody to take her to her own party—"

"She's not that unattractive," Lynn said. "She's changed a lot this year." She could have bitten her tongue for saying so. "There's no reason she can't get her own dates, the same as everybody else. If she doesn't have enough on the ball to get an escort of her own, then she doesn't deserve anything better than sitting home. Imagine, making her mother phone around getting her dates!"

"Oh, come off it," Paul said again, and now he sounded really angry. "You and all the rest of your buddies have always been so darned lofty about Brenda. Maybe she has seemed like a colorless little thing, but with a mother like hers, bossing her around every minute, how could she be anything else? Maybe if you'd ever given her a chance, you'd have found she was a pretty nice kid."

"Oh, stop being so high and mighty!" Lynn snapped. "If you'd rather not go out with me, just say so."

"You know that's not it," Paul said. "We'll go out tomorrow night. For gosh sakes, Lynn, what difference does one night make?"

"Well, it may not make a difference to you," Lynn answered shortly, "but it does to me. If you take Brenda out tonight, Paul Kingsley, you're not going to have another date with me."

Paul was silent a moment. When he finally spoke, his voice was very quiet.

"All right," he said. "All right, if that's the way you want it."

There was a faint click of the receiver.

Lynn said, "Paul—" And then she stopped, realizing in an instant of complete amazement that he had hung up on her.

When the phone rang a few minutes later, she was sure it was Paul, phoning back to apologize. She let the phone ring several times, so as not to seem too eager, and then she picked it up.

"Hello," she said coolly, determined that she was not going to make it easy for him.

"Hello, Lynn?" It was a familiar voice but an unexpected one, and one she had never heard on the telephone before.

It's not Paul, Lynn thought, choking down her disappointment.

She tried to put warmth back into her voice. "Hi, Dirk!"

"Hi! Look—I—er—" He took a deep breath and went on awkwardly. "What I called about—well, I wondered if you were going to be busy tomorrow night?"

Lynn thought about Paul. "We'll go out tomorrow night," he had said. She felt anger rising again within her.

What makes him so sure I'll be here, she thought. Does he think he can date anybody he wants and find me sitting home, waiting for him to come back whenever he wants to? Or does he think I'm so unattractive that nobody else will ask me?

She said, "I don't want to go to Charlie's, Dirk. Or to do any car racing, or double with people like Brad, or—"

"No," Dirk said, "just you and me. We'll go to a show or something—anything you want to do. I—I just want to see you."

Lynn hesitated. She knew her mother disapproved of Dirk. If it had been any other time, she would have taken her mother's opinion into more serious consideration, and said no, especially as she did not particularly want to go out with Dirk herself.

But as it was, Paul's voice still rang in her ears, and her fresh hurt and anger combined to make her tighten her hold on the phone and put a real graciousness into her voice when she said, "Thank you, Dirk, I'd love to go out tomorrow night. What time?"

"About eight?"

"That will be fine. About eight, then."

She placed the phone back on its cradle with a feeling of satisfaction, tinged with desperation.

9

Lynn was sorry afterward. The moment she hung up and turned away from the phone, she thought, what did I do that for? I don't want to go out with Dirk, not when Paul is home. Paul is the only person I want to see.

Her regret increased when Dodie met her in the hall and asked, "Who was on the phone?"

"That's for me to know," Lynn retorted automatically, "and you to find out." But she caught herself, realizing that it was silly to alienate Dodie for no reason at all. "It was Dirk," she added. "He asked me for a date tomorrow night."

"Are you going? Even with Paul home?"

Lynn nodded. "Paul is going out with Brenda Peterson. And if he's dating somebody else, so can I."

Dodie said, "Mother will be livid when she finds out."

"No, she won't." Lynn contradicted her sister. "Mother's never livid; you know that. But I guess she won't be awfully happy." She hesitated. "Say, do you have a date tomorrow?"

"With Ronnie Turner. We're going to the movies."

"Why, that's swell!" Lynn exclaimed. "Why don't we double? Dirk and Ronnie live right near each other, so they must know each other pretty well, and Mother couldn't really object to anything if we were going out together."

"Sorry," Dodie responded breezily, "but Ronnie would

never double with Dirk. He doesn't approve of him."

"You might at least ask him," Lynn said. "Honestly, Dodie, sisters are supposed to help each other out once in a while."

"Don't sound so noble with me!" Dodie retaliated. "Since when have you felt so strongly about this sisters-stick-together business? There have been plenty of times when we could have doubled, if you'd just said the word, times when Paul had a car and my date didn't, or when there was an extra fellow you might have gotten me a date with. But oh no, I was 'baby sister' then. Now, all of a sudden, it would be to your advantage to double with me and you think it would be a fine thing! Well, no thanks."

She turned and started down the hall. As Lynn stood, gazing after her sister, beneath her anger there was the sneaking knowledge that Dodie was justified in what she said. There had been many times when she had refused to double with Dodie on the grounds that she was too young.

As she reached the head of the stairs, however, Dodie turned back.

"Look," she said, "I'm not just being mean about this. Ronnie really wouldn't double with Dirk, no matter what I said. We've talked about him before, and Ronnie feels pretty strongly about him. He doesn't like the way he acts or the kind of crowd he runs around with or the way he doesn't do any work after school when his dad needs help. I wouldn't even want to *ask* him about doubling."

"O.K.," Lynn said. "O.K., we'll get along just fine without you. Better, in fact. Dirk probably doesn't like Ronnie, either."

"No," Dodie agreed placidly, "he probably doesn't."

The next morning, after breakfast Paul came over, and again Lynn wished she had not agreed to go out with Dirk, for when she saw him standing in the doorway, she felt her anger slipping away.

"Hi!" he said. "Are you going to shut the door in my face?"

"No," Lynn answered. "Of course not. I don't shut doors in people's faces."

"Even people who hang up on you?"

"Even them." She smiled at him in spite of herself. "Come on in, Paul."

He came in, regarding her hesitantly. When he spoke, his voice sounded very young. "You're not mad any more?"

Lynn shook her head. "I guess not. I mean, not the way I was yesterday."

"Well, I'm glad of that," Paul said in relief. "I'm sorry I hung up on you. I guess I got kind of mad myself. It just wasn't like you to act that way. I mean, gosh, it wasn't as though I really wanted to take Brenda. It was just one of those things you get pushed into doing and then can't get out of again. Besides, she isn't such a bad kid. She only needs people to like her."

Lynn choked down the sharp comment that sprang to the tip of her tongue. Instead she asked, "How was the party last night?"

"It was a good one," Paul said easily, seating himself on the sofa and relaxing against the upholstered arm. "All the gang was there. There was a really great orchestra, and they had the club decorated to beat the band. I hear the Presentation Ball next spring is going to be the party to end all parties. They've already hired an orchestra to come in from out of town to play for it."

"Are you—" Lynn hated to ask the question, but she had to. "Are you very sorry I'm not a debutante?"

"Sure, I'm sorry," Paul answered frankly. "It's a darned shame we can't go to all these things, but you certainly couldn't be a debutante and have your father campaigning against it at the same time."

"What do you mean, campaigning against it?" Lynn asked in surprise. "You mean, Daddy's been talking to people about it?"

"You mean, you didn't know?" Now it was Paul's turn to look surprised. "Why, my dad said your father gave a twenty-minute talk in Rotary Club the other day, all about how having debutantes in a place this size would divide the town into classes and wreck the whole democratic attitude. He said the whole purpose of a public high school is to help kids make friends from all kinds of backgrounds, and having chosen girls make their debuts would destroy that ideal entirely. Dad said it was quite a speech. He said he thought your father had something there. Of course, some of the other men disagreed with him, but they were mostly the ones with daughters who were debutantes."

"How do you feel about it?" Lynn asked. "Do you think Daddy's right?"

"Yes," Paul said slowly, "I guess he is, really. It's hard on you, though, having to miss the parties."

"And on you," Lynn added. "Paul—" Now that he had not asked, she could offer it to him. "Paul, would you like to—to—be free to go to the parties? I mean, without me?"

"Oh, don't be silly!" Paul exclaimed impatiently. "I don't

care that much about parties. You and I will have fun during the holidays, and nuts to everybody else."

"You really mean it?"

"Sure." Paul reached over and took her hand. "Last night as I was all set to leave, Mrs. Peterson got me off in a corner and asked me if I'd take Brenda to tonight's party, a treasure hunt of some kind. She said the same guy usually escorted the same girl to all the holiday parties, and she was counting on me to take Brenda. You know what I told her? I said, 'I'm sorry, I've got a date tomorrow night with Lynn Chambers.'" He grinned at her. "So start thinking what you want to do."

"I—tonight?" Lynn's throat was dry. "Why—I didn't know we had a date tonight"

"Well, of course, we do. Hey—" His blue eyes darkened. "This isn't a run-around, is it Lynn? I told you on the phone that we'd go out tonight. I thought you said you weren't still mad."

"I'm not," Lynn said quickly. "It's not that I'm mad. It's just—well, I already have a date for tonight."

"You, what?" Paul stared at her. "Oh, come off it Lynn, I said I'm sorry. What more do you want me to do, grovel on the floor, begging you to go out with me?"

"No, I *do* have a date," Lynn insisted. "I'm sorry. I wish I didn't. It's just that yesterday, right after I talked to you, while I was still angry, Dirk Masters called and—"

"Dirk Masters!" Paul exclaimed, jerking himself erect "Don't tell me you're dating that guy! Look here, Lynn, you can just call him back and tell him nothing doing. You've got date with me for tonight and that's that."

"I'm sorry," Lynn said again. "I would if I could but

Paul, I can't. I promised him. I can't break it now, any more than you could break your date with Brenda last night."

"It's another thing entirely," Paul said stiffly, getting to his feet. "Brenda's a nice kid who needed an escort to a party. Dirk's a tough little smart aleck who's never been out with a decent girl in his life. If you think I'll let you go out with a guy like that—"

"I'm afraid you don't have much to say about it," Lynn said shortly. "What makes you think you can boss me around, telling me what I can and can't do? Just because I'm wearing your ring doesn't mean you own me, body and soul."

"Well, you won't be wearing my ring for long," Paul said angrily, "if you don't start acting like your old self again. I know darned well the only reason you are going out with Dirk is to get even with me for taking Brenda to the party. Well, I told you I was sorry for that. I refused to take her out again. I don't know what else you expect me to do about it."

"I don't expect you to do anything!" snapped Lynn.

"Well, fine," Paul said. "Because I don't intend to. The next step's up to you. I've got some work to do on my car, before I can go any place tonight, so I'm going to go home and get at it. If you want to go out with me, you give me a call before noon. If I don't hear from you by then, I'm going to call Mrs. Peterson back and tell her I will take Brenda tonight."

"Which is probably what you want to do, anyway," Lynn said bitterly.

But this time Paul did not even bother to answer.

Now everything is even worse than it was before, Lynn thought miserably, as she dressed for her date with Dirk that evening.

She had been sorely tempted to phone Paul. He had said he would wait for her until noon. All it would have taken to make things right between them was one little phone call.

But I couldn't, Lynn told herself now, adjusting the belt to her dress and giving herself a last disinterested glance in the mirror. It's not just a matter of pride. Paul is wrong, but I don't mind being the one to try to patch things up. That's what a girl is for. I couldn't call off the date with Dirk, though, not after I promised him. Surely Paul could have understood that.

She thought about Dirk and the way it had been between them that night at his home—the way he had looked at her for the first time, a long look, without the usual mockery or defiance in his eyes; the sound of his voice when he said, "About the other evening—I'm sorry."

She thought, I couldn't break a date with him. Not after that. Why, that night we were almost friends. If I do something to hurt him now, all that will be lost. Any influence I have over him would be gone. I'd never be able to get through to him again and help him to be the kind of person he can be, if he tries.

And even through her misery about Paul, she felt a slight stirring of excitement at the idea of having the power to reform Dirk.

She tried to put Paul out of her mind as she went down the stairs to answer the doorbell.

As it happened, it was not Dirk who stood in the living

room, talking to her parents, but Ronnie Turner. He stood up as Lynn entered. It was the first time Lynn had met him, and she was surprised at what a nice-looking boy he was, with his sandy hair and straightforward eyes. She knew he was several years younger than Dirk, but when she shook hands with him, she had the feeling that somehow he was much older. There was a steadiness about him and a kind of strength. When he and Dodie left together, he put his hand on her arm with a protective little gesture that made Dr. Chambers turn to his wife with a smile.

"Nice boy," he commented briefly.

And she said, "Yes, I think he'll be good for Dodie."

A few moments later, the bell sounded again, and it was Dirk.

He was neatly dressed, with his hair carefully combed back from his forehead, instead of tumbled forward in its usual rakish manner. He was handsome, Lynn thought, as soon as she saw him—handsomer by far than Ronnie, or even than Paul. But she had the feeling when they left the house that her father would not turn to her mother after they were gone and say, "Nice boy." She wondered exactly what he would say. It was hard to guess.

As they reached the street, Dirk took her arm and steered her to a car parked there.

"Brad's car again?" Lynn asked. She could not keep the disapproval out of her voice.

"Sure," Dirk said, a hint of the old mockery back in his voice as he climbed in beside her. "You don't feel like walking, do you? You know, we all can't have our own private limousine, like some guys I know."

"Maybe not," Lynn said, ignoring the implication, "but

I wouldn't have minded taking the bus. They're kind of fun, really. I'd rather that than have you have to borrow a car from somebody like Brad."

Dirk started up the engine and drove down the Hill Road. "What do you have against Brad? You've hardly met him."

"Anne has told me about him."

"Oh, Anne! Well, she's just got a kind of thing on about him because he's older than the other guys and has been around more. Anne's like that." He turned toward her with a sudden, almost pleading look. "Look, let's not argue about anything tonight. I mean, I'll try my darndest to act like you want me to, and you—well, why don't you try to like me. I mean, really try."

"That won't be hard," Lynn said. "I do like you. I'm sorry if I started right off being critical."

Dirk pulled to a halt at the entrance to the River Road.

"What would you like to do? I know you don't want to go any place like Charlie's. What about a movie?"

"Oh, I don't know," Lynn answered. "I guess a movie would be fine." She did not feel particularly like seeing a movie, but she couldn't think of anything else.

The movie, when they got there, was a dull one. Dirk did not suggest sitting in the balcony, probably because the rest of his crowd would be located there and he had promised Lynn that they would not be with *them* tonight. Instead, they sat down in front, in the only available seats, a little too close to the screen. They arrived in the middle of the picture, and it was almost over before Lynn began to understand what it was all about and by the time she did understand, she was too bored with it to care. It seemed much later than ten o'clock when they finally left the theater and got into the car.

Dirk asked, "Where to now?"

He sounded a little desperate. Lynn knew he was trying to give her a nice evening, and yet somehow it just wasn't panning out. All she wanted to do was go home and go to bed. The scene with Paul that morning had left her spent and exhausted emotionally, but of course, Dirk had no way of knowing this. If she asked to go home now, he would think it was because of him, and with all the effort he was making, she did not want him to think that Lynn suggested, "Why don't we just drive a little while?"

Dirk seemed pleased. "O.K. That's what I wanted to do myself, only I didn't think you'd want to."

He drove slowly. When he passed the entrance to the Hill Road, Lynn could see the Peterson house, brightly lighted with all the gaiety of a party. There was a string of cars parked outside, leading all the way down the street and several others were just pulling up. A crowd of young people stood on the sidewalk outside the house, gathered around what must have been their collection of "treasures." Lynn caught sight of a broad-shouldered boy bent a little forward, talking to a girl. In the darkness, she could not tell who it was, but there was something about the way the boy was standing, with his head cocked a little to one side, that made her think of Paul.

She thought it could be Paul! And the girl could be Brenda! And if it isn't—well, what difference does it make? He's there with her some place.

There was an ache in her chest almost too great to bear. Oh, Paul, she thought miserably. Oh, Paul!

Dirk was giving her a funny look. "Is anything the matter?"

"What?" Lynn shook her head. "Oh, no. I was just noticing the party at the Petersons'. It's supposed to be a treasure hunt tonight. It looks like it might be a good one."

"Oh!" Dirk was still looking at her sideways. "Your fellow—the one you go with—the Kingsley boy. How come you're not going out with him? He's home now, isn't he?"

"Yes, he's home," Lynn said wearily. "He might as well not be, though. All we've done since he got here is fight."

Dirk said, "Are you wearing his ring, by any chance?"

Lynn put her hand up and felt for the chain. It was there, as it always was, light and warm around her neck, with the weight of the ring swinging beneath her blouse. She thought of Paul's words when he gave it to her. "You're my girl. We've got something between us worth hanging onto."

But we don't, she thought miserably. Not any more. I'm not his girl, and we don't have anything between us at all.

She reached up with both hands and unfastened the little chain and drew it from around her neck. Then she opened her pocketbook and dumped both chain and ring inside.

"There," she said quietly. And then, suddenly, through the calm and composure, came the tears. Her eyes stung with the salty drops. She shut them tightly, but the tears pushed their way out from under her lashes.

Dirk said, "Don't, please!" He pulled the car to the side of the road and shut off the engine. He said, "Please, Lynn—"

He moved over and put his arm around her, not the way

he had before, but with a hesitant gentleness. Lynn pressed her face against his shoulder, trying to stop the tears. But she could not. They came anyway.

"I'm s-sorry," she sobbed. "I'm s-so ashamed of myself. Here I am out with y-you—and you've been so nice to me—and I act like this. But oh, Dirk, when you go with somebody—and he's really special—and then you break up—"

"I know," Dirk said quietly. "I know what it is to—to care about somebody—and not have it work. Go ahead and cry, if it'll make you feel any better. I don't care."

And now, because it was all right to cry, Lynn immediately found that she no longer wanted to. The pain was still there, and the emptiness, but there were no more tears. She sat very quietly, acutely conscious of Dirk's arm around her shoulders. She felt as though it did not belong there, but there was not much she could do about it. And it was comforting, in a way. She let herself relax against him, and he tightened his arm a little, and she found it was really not unpleasant at all.

"I've got a job," Dirk said suddenly. "In Burton's Garage, after school and on Saturdays."

"You do?" Lynn said, surprised. "Why, that's grand."

"I thought you'd be glad," Dirk said. He hesitated, and when he spoke again, his voice was a little shaky. "Look, Lynn, I know I'm not the kind of guy you're used to going with. Not like Kingsley, for instance. It's not just that I don't have the things they have, the nice cars and coming from the Hill and all. I know I've done some things I shouldn't have done. I don't know how to say this—"

"Don't," Lynn said, suddenly nervous. "Don't go on,

Dirk. You don't have to say this to me."

"Yes, I do. I want to." His words came out in a kind of rush. "Look, Lynn, I'm going to try. I swear I am. I'm going to keep straight and go around with the right kind of fellows and keep out of trouble. I want to be the kind of guy you'd be proud to go with."

"Dirk; don't!" Lynn reached up, trying to put her hand over his lips. This was what she had wanted, that he should reform because of her, and yet, now that he was actually saying it, the responsibility was oddly terrifying.

"No," she said, "not just for me. For yourself, for your father, for Anne—"

"For you," Dirk said. He moved his arm from around her shoulders, and Lynn drew away in relief.

Dirk reached forward and opened the glove compartment of the car. He took out a small cardboard box.

"This is for you," he said. "A Christmas present."

"Why, it's not Christmas yet," Lynn reminded him nervously. She took the box in her hands. "Do you—do you want me to open it?"

Dirk nodded. "I know it's not Christmas but I want you to have it now. Especially since you're not wearing that chain and ring any longer."

The little box was not wrapped. Lynn lifted the lid easily. She caught her breath as she saw the string of pearls which lay inside.

"Oh, Dirk, how beautiful!" And in almost the same breath, "I can't accept anything like this!"

"Sure you can. It's just a Christmas present. All guys give their girls Christmas presents."

Lynn opened her mouth to say, "But I'm not your girl.

And even if I were—" But she had no chance to shape the words, for Dirk was still talking, his voice very earnest, an open, defenseless look on his face that made him look very, very young.

"This was my mother's. Her folks gave it to her on her twenty-first birthday, and Dad would never let her sell it, even when the going was toughest. He said he wanted her to have *something* nice, even if he wasn't the one to give it to her. After she married Dad, her folks never gave her anything again." He took a deep breath. "She left it to me. She left the rest of her stuff to Anne, but this was for me, so I'd have something to give to the 'right girl' when I found her. I didn't have the nerve to give it to you before, so I thought I'd keep it for Christmas. Everybody gives things at Christmas. And now you're not going with Kingsley any longer—"

His voice broke, and he leaned forward so that his face was buried against her hair.

"I know I can't give you the kind of things he must have been able to. But I want you to have this. Please—I'll probably never have anything as nice to give you again."

Lynn closed her eyes and leaned her head back against the back of the seat.

She thought, what should I do? I know I shouldn't accept a present like this, especially from Dirk. I'm not in love with him, and it would not mean what he wants it to mean, and it's much too expensive a present. But how can I say no? It would hurt him terribly.

"All right," she said at last. "I will keep it. And thank you so much, Dirk. It's one of the most beautiful things I have ever owned."

He put his arms around her, and she knew he was going to kiss her, and she knew she could not draw away. Not now. Not even with the tears about Paul not quite dry on her cheeks.

"I love you," Dirk whispered. "Please, please try to love me too."

There was something terrifying in having a boy like this, a hard, tough boy, suddenly weak before her, clinging to her in a kind of desperation.

She thought, I don't want this. Please, please, I don't want this.

But she sat very still beside him, and when he kissed her, she wanted to cry—for him, and for her, too. And she thought Paul—Paul—

10

The house was very quiet when Lynn got in. The only downstairs light was the one left burning for her in the hall, and she realized with a start that her mother and father must already be in bed.

Her first feeling was one of relief. She was sure that something of the night's happenings must show on her face, and she was glad that she would not have to face her mother until morning. On second thought, however, she almost wished her mother was up waiting for her, for then she would be forced to show her the necklace and tell her about the evening, and somehow the telling of it would be a relief.

She climbed the stairs slowly, hesitating beside her parents' half-open door.

"Lynn?" It was her father's voice, muffled with sleep.

"Yes, Daddy."

"Didn't want to go to sleep till you got in. You're late, Daughter."

"Yes, I know." She searched desperately in her mind for some excuse. She could think of none. "We—we just got talking, and I lost track of time. I'm sorry."

"If you're mature enough to be dating, you're mature enough not to lose track of time." Her father yawned. "Oh, well, we'll hash it over in the morning. Get to bed now."

"Yes, Daddy. Good night."

Lynn continued down the hall, grateful that her father had been too tired for a real scolding this evening. By morning, he might have forgotten the hour she arrived home.

And then, at the entrance to their shared bathroom, she ran into the one person she definitely did not want to see—her sister.

"Hi!" Dodie said "Have you seen Daddy? He's simply livid because you're so late getting home. What on earth were you doing so late?"

"None of your business," Lynn retorted. And then, "What are *you* doing up, anyway, if it's so late?"

"Putting up my hair," Dodie said. "It always takes me a long time, and Ronnie likes it curly." She gave her sister a sharp glance. "You've been crying."

Lynn knew it was useless to try to evade the issue. Nothing ever escaped Dodie's prying eyes. Too late, she glanced down and saw that she was still holding the cardboard box in her hands.

Dodie had, of course, seen this too. Her gaze fastened on it and then traveled up again, to focus on her sister's face, and, to Lynn's surprise, there was no mischief in it.

"Whatever it is that's the matter," Dodie said, "would you like to tell me about it? I won't say anything to Mother or Daddy, if you don't want me to. I'll just listen, and maybe I can help you work it out. I'm pretty good at solving things."

To her own surprise, Lynn found herself nodding in agreement. "Yes," she said, "I guess I would like to talk about it."

"Come on then," Dodie said, her usual briskness returning. "We can go in my room, where we can talk without waking up everybody else in the house."

Still a little bewildered by the course of events, Lynn followed her sister into her bedroom.

Dodie's room was like Dodie herself, bright and neat and animated. In contrast to the gentle pastels of Lynn's room, Dodie's red and white plaid curtains seemed to be made for blowing in a wind, and there was a smart, tailored look to the straight white bedspread and the red and gold band around the apron on the dressing table. Lynn realized with surprise that she had very seldom been in her sister's room. It was almost like visiting with a stranger. She had an impulse to say, "How attractive everything is! How neat you keep your things!" but she restrained herself. Instead, she sat down awkwardly on the corner of the bed, while Dodie seated herself in the white and gold armchair.

"O.K.," she said, "begin."

"I don't quite know how to begin," Lynn said awkwardly. "Everything's such a mess. You know about Paul, and then tonight with Dirk—I couldn't hurt him, not after he's changed so much, just for my sake. I didn't know what to do!"

"Look," Dodie said briskly, "start with first things first For instance, what's in the box?"

"A necklace." Lynn opened the lid and drew forth the string of pearls.

Dodie caught her breath. "Golly Moses, Lynn! Are they real?"

"I think so," Lynn said. "They were Dirk's mother's. That's one thing that made it so hard—I *couldn't* say 'no' to something that meant so much to him. But the way he gave it to me—the things he said—I feel so responsible—"

She went on with the story, discovering it was easier and easier to find words as she watched the sympathetic expression on Dodie's face. She found herself telling even more than she had intended to, telling the little things—how she had seen the treasure-hunt party, the boy she thought might be Paul, the way she had cried against Dirk's shoulder, the things he had said and the things she had answered.

"So," she finished finally, "there just wasn't anything else to do. I couldn't refuse to take them, could I?"

Dodie was silent a moment. Then she said, 'It's a real problem, isn't it? It's easy for me to give advice, because I'm not part of it. If I were, I don't know what I'd do."

"Well, as the disinterested party, what do you think?"

Lynn found herself waiting in real anxiety for Dodie's answer.

"It seems to me there's just one thing you can do. Give the necklace back and break with Dirk just as fast as you can."

"But I can't!" Lynn exclaimed. "Not after tonight. It's too late for that."

Dodie shook her head. "It's too late for anything else. The way it looks to me, this thing is snowballing into something that's going to be too big to deal with, if you don't cut it off right now. Dirk isn't just a little kid with his first puppy love; he's a couple of years older than you are, practically a man, and he's been around and he's serious. And you're not." She hesitated. "That is right, isn't it Lynn? You're not in love with him, too?"

"Of course not," Lynn asserted. "But I like him, and

I don't want to hurt him. And if being in love with me is going to change him—to make a better person of him—"

"Then what's going to happen when he wants you to go steady with him? Are you going to go along with that too, because you think it will help him?"

"I told you, I'm not in love with him. Of course, I wouldn't go steady with him. But I guess I see what you mean. I'd have to break off with him then, and by that time he would have come to count on me more and more, and it would be much worse." She sighed and got slowly to her feet "Thanks, Dodie. I feel better now. I guess I did just want to talk it out with somebody. I see now that there's just one thing I can do."

She hesitated by her sister's chair. She had an impulse to give her a quick hug of gratitude. But Dodie was not the kind of a girl who hugged people, so Lynn merely smiled instead.

"Thanks," she said again.

"Think nothing of it." Dodie said briskly. "Little sisters make pretty good sounding boards."

"Big ones do, too," Lynn said softly. "Remember that. You may have your own problems one of these days."

"I probably will."

Dodie smiled at her, and Lynn smiled back, and there was a closeness between them that had never been there before. For the first time, it seemed as though they were more than just sisters. They were actually friends.

When she lay in bed that night Lynn thought about this some more. It was strange the way, when she had needed her, Dodie had been there. Talking to her had made the problem with Dirk seem less tremendous, more a size that could be coped with. What had happened to Dodie tonight to make her so much warmer and friendlier?

And the answer came to her in something little Janie had said one time— "If Dodie cares about you and if you need her, she will do anything in the world for you." Thinking back on it, Lynn saw that this was true. To the people who needed her, to Janie who could not pass her Latin course without help, to Ronnie who had first come to her attention when he was struggling to handle a job and three little brothers at the same time, Dodie had given of herself warmly and freely. And tonight, for the very first time, Lynn had needed her sister. And Dodie had been there.

The new relationship with Dodie, however, was the only bright note in the Christmas holidays. The next week passed slowly and miserably. Lynn found herself jumping each time the telephone rang and holding her breath whenever anyone else answered, desperate with the hope that it might be Paul.

But it never was.

Dirk phoned twice, and both times Lynn found an excuse not to go out with him, once because she had a headache and the second time because it was her mother's birthday.

"You can't keep doing this indefinitely," Dodie remarked, after Lynn had hung up from the second call. "It's not going to be Mother's birthday forever, you know. One of these days, you're going to have to see him and give him back the necklace, and putting it off isn't making it any easier."

"I know," Lynn sighed. "I guess I'm just a coward. I hate the thought of a scene."

Dodie nodded, understandingly. "I understand." She

gave her sister a sharp glance. "What about you and Paul? Is that completely over?"

Lynn felt the sinking sensation in her stomach that always came with the mention of Paul.

"I guess it is. He hasn't called, and Ernie says he's been taking Brenda to all the debutante parties. That pasty-faced little Brenda! I guess she's pretty proud of herself, having got her claws into Paul. And all the time she looks so innocent."

Dodie nodded sympathetically. "I always said she was a drip."

Nancy, however, had a different remark to make when Lynn mentioned the situation to her. Although Nancy was active in all the debutante functions and had much less time to spend with Lynn these days, she still dropped over fairly often. Lynn could not help wondering whether it was because of their friendship or because she was going with Ernie. Either way, she was grateful for this one tie with old times.

"Can you imagine," Lynn said, "making her mother phone Paul to force him to take her out? Isn't that nerve for you?"

Nancy was silent a moment. Then she said, "I just can't believe that, Lynn. I've come to know Brenda pretty well since she became a debutante, and I don't think she's like that."

"You mean you don't believe me!" Lynn was stunned.

"Oh, Lynn! I believe that Mrs. Peterson called—it's just like something she would do; but I can't believe that Brenda knew about it. You should see her with Paul, Lynn. She's just as sparkly and excited. I think he must be the first boy who has ever paid attention to her. I don't think she knows about her mother calling at all."

"You mean she thinks he just threw me over in order to go out with her?"

Nancy flushed. "I don't mean exactly that, either. I just don't think she knows her mother had anything to do with it." She hesitated. "You know, Lynn, you shouldn't have been so mad at Paul for taking Brenda to that first dance. I'm sure he didn't think it would hurt you. He just thought she was in trouble, not having an escort, and he was going to help her out."

"But why?" Lynn snapped back. "Of all the boys in town, why did Paul feel he had to be the one to help her?"

"Because he's like that," Nancy answered quietly. "He always has been; you know that. Remember how you met him in the first place, when he was helping Ernie make the team? He didn't have to do that any more than he had to help Brenda. It's just the way he is."

Lynn nodded, her eyes suddenly full of tears.

"I know," she said finally.

It was this very trait in Paul which had endeared him to her in the first place. The warm, easy friendliness with which he faced the whole world.

And I was his girl, she thought miserably. I wore his ring.

At the thought of the ring, another idea occurred to her. She suddenly realized that she ought to return the ring to Paul. He's too polite to come and ask for it, she told herself, and he might want it back. He might want it now, before he goes back to college.

And then still another idea, one she could not bear

to put into words, trembled at the brink of her mind—he might want the ring to give to Brenda.

Before the ache could get any worse and perhaps she would not be able to force herself to do it, she ran up the stairs to her room and got the ring out of her purse and sealed it in an envelope. She wrote, "For Paul Kingsley" on the front and, that evening, she gave the envelope to Ernie.

"Here," she said, "at the party tonight give this to Paul, will you?"

Ernie nodded absent-mindedly and started to put the envelope in his pocket. Then he hesitated, letting his fingers touch the knobby little lump inside. He glanced up at his sister questioningly.

"You sure you want me to, Sis? You sure this is how you want it?"

Lynn answered, "This is how *he* wants it."

"I don't know." Ernie frowned. "I think you're giving up too easily. That little Peterson gal—well, I didn't used to think she amounted to anything. I guess nobody did. But since the debutante parties started, she's been like another girl, kind of peppy and bright looking, almost pretty. Not as pretty as you are, of course, but the way she looks at Paul— well, it's fairly easy to see, she's falling for him hard." He stopped at the hurt in Lynn's eyes. "I'm sorry, Sis. I didn't mean to make you feel any worse. I just want you to realize how things are. I don't know if Paul's fallen for her or not, but if he hasn't—and then you give back his ring—and Brenda's right there, thinking he's wonderful—well, it's just asking for it. You just might be giving it a push."

He was looking at her with such brotherly concern that

Lynn felt the tears starting again.

This is just ridiculous, she thought. All I do is cry these days. I don't think I've done so much weeping and wailing since I was a brand new baby.

"I know what I'm doing," she said. "If Paul wants me to have the ring, he can come and tell me so. But he doesn't. I'm sure of that."

Ernie shrugged, his duty done. "O.K., Sis, if that's the way you want it."

That evening, however, Lynn found she could not sleep. She lay awake until very late, when she heard Ernie's footsteps in the hall. He was humming one of the popular dance tunes, one that centered around a girl's name, but, when she listened more closely, Lynn heard him singing, "Nancy— Nancy," instead.

She got up softly and opened the door into the hall.

"Ern?"

"Oh, hi, Sis! What are you doing up?"

"I was in bed. I just heard you and thought—" She swallowed whatever pride she had. "Did you give Paul the envelope?"

"Yes. I saw him during one of the intermissions."

"What did he say?"

"Nothing," Ernie said. "He didn't say anything. He just took it and put it in his pocket and walked away."

"He didn't even open it?"

"He didn't have to," Ernie told her. "He just kind of felt the shape of it and put it in his pocket. He knew what was in it." He reached over and gave her shoulder an awkward pat. "Don't brood about it Sis. What's over is over. Go on back to bed and get some sleep."

"O.K.," Lynn said wearily. "Good night Ernie, and thank you."

And strangely enough, when she went back to bed, she did sleep, more soundly than she had for a long time. It was a heavy sleep, and when she awoke the next morning, she saw by the bedroom clock that it was almost noon. She dragged herself to a sitting position, feeling more tired than she had when she went to bed.

There was a light rap at her door.

"Lynn, are you awake yet?" It was Dodie.

"Yes," Lynn said dully, "what is it?"

'Telephone." Dodie opened the door and thrust in her head. "Don't look so eager. It's just Dirk. He wants you to go out with him tonight. He says he's been trying to get you all week."

"Oh, dear!" Lynn said wearily. "I suppose I'll have to talk to him."

She swung her legs over the side of the bed and stood up. The floor seemed very far away. She moved uncertainly toward the door.

Dodie was watching her, a worried expression on her face. "Lynn, is anything the matter? You look so funny."

"Nothing's the matter," Lynn said. "You know how heavy you feel when you've slept too long."

She went into the hall. The telephone was off the hook, lying on the table. She picked it up.

"Hello, Dirk."

"Hi! How about taking in a movie tonight? Brad's letting me use his car."

"No," Lynn said. "I'm sorry, Dirk. I can't."

"What do you mean, you can't?" There was a funny note

in his voice. "I've been calling you for a couple of weeks now, and every time I ask you out, you can't go. What's the reason this time?"

"I—I—" No appropriate reason came to mind. Lynn leaned wearily against the wall, and suddenly it was too much trouble to go on making excuses any longer.

"It's not that I can't," she said. "It's that I don't think I should. It wouldn't be fair, to you or to me."

"Why wouldn't it be fair?" His voice was sharper. "What are you trying to say?"

"That I'm not in love with you," Lynn said, "and that I never will be. I like you, Dirk, so much, and I'm so touched that you wanted me to have the necklace, but I should never have taken it and I can't keep it now. I hate hurting you, but I can't just lead you on and keep dating you and pretending there's a chance I might get to care, when really there isn't."

Dirk was silent a moment. Then he said, "O.K., O.K., I get it. I should have known it would be like this, with you being from the Hill and all. But I let myself start thinking you were different, that it didn't matter to you about a guy's background. I was pretty dumb, wasn't I? Because you're just like all the rest of them—"

"Oh, Dirk, don't!" Lynn interrupted miserably. "That's not the way it is at all. It's Paul, that's all, just Paul. If you were from the Hill and Paul wasn't, it would still be Paul. I don't know why. You can't explain those things; they just happen. I like you, Dirk. I wish we could be friends."

Lynn braced herself against the torrent of bitterness she was sure would come. She need not have.

When Dirk spoke again, it was quietly. "No," he said. "No thanks, Princess, I don't think I want to be friends."

There was a faint click as he hung up.

So it is over, Lynn thought, almost with relief. Dirk—Paul—everything, all over.

She turned back toward her room, and suddenly her legs doubled beneath her.

"Mother!" she cried, grabbing for the door handle for support. "Mother!"

"Something *is* the matter!" Dodie was beside her. "Here, lean on me and I'll get you over to the bed. Then I'll find Mother for you."

Leaning heavily on her sister, Lynn stumbled forward into her bedroom. She tumbled onto the bed and pressed her face into the cool pillow. She could hear Dodie's voice ringing through the house.

"Mother! Mother, come quick! Something's the matter with Lynn!"

A moment later, Mrs. Chambers was beside the bed.

"What is it dear? What's wrong?" She laid her hand against Lynn's forehead. "Why, you're burning up with fever! You stay right here while I call your father at the office and have him come home and look at you."

An hour later, after Dr. Chambers had come and gone, Lynn found herself still in bed. She'd had a shot of penicillin and several small bottles of pills were lined up on the nearby table.

"It's just flu," her father had said. "It's been going around lately, and, to tell the truth, Daughter, you've been looking pretty run-down these past few weeks. After you're through with this siege, I'm going to start you in on some iron pills and vitamins."

"She has been looking pale and tired," Mrs. Chambers agreed. "I've been noticing it, too." She gave her daughter's hand a gentle pat. "You just stay in bed a few days, and we'll get you back to normal again. Isn't it lucky we have a doctor in the family?"

"Very lucky," Lynn said weakly.

Some time later, Dodie stuck her head in again.

"I hear you've got the flu bug. I won't come in because I don't want to catch it, not when I have a date with Ronnie for Midnight Mass Christmas night. But about Dirk—did you talk to him? Is everything all right?"

"All right?" Lynn said. "No, it's not all right. He's hurt and furious and will probably hate me as long as he lives. Dirk—Paul—everything is such a horrid, confused mess! I wonder if I'll ever feel really happy again."

"Oh, don't be silly!" Dodie said with a touch of her old impatience.

Lynn sighed and turned her face to the wall. Sleep came sweeping over her like a dead weight that had been lifted for a moment and was now settling again. She did not even hear the door close as Dodie went out.

11

Christmas got lost that year. There was a tree, of course, just as there always was, and there were gifts, but Lynn did not feel up to enjoying them. Dr. Chambers proclaimed her well enough to move down to the sofa in the living room for Christmas morning, and she tried to enter wholeheartedly into the festivities, as she had on all previous Christmases, but the effort was more exhausting than stimulating. By the time the last present was unwrapped, she was more than ready to return to bed and to stay there the rest of the morning.

In the afternoon, Nancy stopped over with her gift, a bright plaid scarf. They talked a few minutes, but then Nancy said she had to leave. "There's so much to crowd into so little time," she explained. "The first thing tomorrow morning, there's a rehearsal for the charity fashion show. It's only a week off, and we want it to be perfect. Otherwise, we couldn't charge people two dollars apiece, just for watching it."

Nancy looked pretty, her red hair shining and soft around her face, her blue eyes glowing. She was wearing the lavender sweater set that Ernie had given her. He had saved for months to buy it and had gone to pick it out by himself. Lynn was amazed that it was such a pretty shade and good fit. She had never realized her brother had such good taste.

"Do you have to go so soon?" Lynn asked, with disappointment in her voice. "At least stay a few minutes longer and tell me about the fashion show. All I know about it is what Dodie gleaned from Janie over the telephone."

"It's going to be fun," Nancy said, settling herself again in her chair. "The debutantes are going to do the modeling, and the clothes are out of this world! They're the early spring, resort-wear fashions, expensive as the dickens and just dreamy. And then, as a finale, we're all going to model the evening gowns we're going to wear to make our debuts."

"I imagine you'll have a good audience for that kind of a show," Lynn said, trying to keep the longing from her voice. Her height and graceful carriage had always made her sought after as a model in local fashion shows, and it hurt to be left out of this one.

"I imagine we will," Nancy agreed. "Especially since the proceeds will go to the Rivertown Memorial Hospital. By the way, has your father made any comment about that?"

"No," Lynn said in surprise. "Not that I know of. Why?"

"Well," Nancy told her, "it was Mrs. Peterson's idea that the money go to the hospital, instead of to some charity. Everybody knows that your father has been against having debutantes, and I should think it would put him in a rather difficult position. He's Chief of Staff at the hospital, isn't he?"

"Yes," Lynn said, "he is. I hadn't really thought about it, but it *will* be a little awkward for him to accept the donation and—" Suddenly her eyes blazed with anger. "Why, Mrs. Peterson planned it that way, didn't she? Deliberately planned it, just to embarrass Daddy! What a spiteful, horrid thing to do!"

"Oh, it's not that bad," Nancy said soothingly. "The hospital needs the money. They'll be glad to get it, whatever the source."

"But it's such a petty thing to do!" Lynn exclaimed. "Not that the money won't be welcome, but I'm sure that's not why Mrs. Peterson has decided to donate it. It's her way of getting back at Daddy."

"I've got to go." Nancy jumped to her feet. "I shouldn't have come, Lynn. I didn't mean to get you so upset."

"I'm sorry, Nan, I shouldn't have got so mad. I don't have to take it out on *you*." Lynn gave her friend an apologetic smile. "I'm glad you did come; I haven't seen anybody outside of the family for days. And thanks so much for the scarf— I love it."

"And thank you for the record," Nancy said, glancing down fondly at the package Lynn had given her. "Merry Christmas! And get well soon!"

"Merry Christmas!" Lynn echoed, trying to get some of the gaiety of the season into her voice. If it did not come off quite right, at least it sounded better than it had before. "Merry Christmas, and have fun this week."

With Nancy gone, the house seemed suddenly very empty and quiet. Lynn picked up a book and laid it down again. She found she felt too nervous and edgy to read. After a few minutes, she got up and wandered down the hall, looking for someone to talk to.

She paused at Dodie's door. "Hi! Are you going out?"

"Yes." Dodie was in the process of pulling a half slip over her head. Now she jerked it back up, so she could look at her sister. "What's the matter? You sound burned up about something."

"Not burned up," Lynn said shortly. "Just irritated. Nancy's been telling me about the fashion show, and I know it's a grand thing that the hospital is getting the money, and yet Mrs. Peterson is only doing it to be nasty, and—"

"And at the same time," Dodie said flatly, "you'd like to be taking part in the show yourself."

"No! That's not it at all!" Lynn felt her face growing hot. "It's just—well—" She stopped, ashamed of herself. "Yes," she said in a lower voice, "I guess you're right. I do wish I were in it. Oh, Dodie, I feel so—so—left out of things!" She changed the subject abruptly. "Where are you going?"

"Skating." Dodie gave her a long look. "Listen, Lynn, I don't mean to stick my nose into your business, but there's something I've been wanting to say to you for quite a while, and I guess maybe now is the time to say it."

"Yes?" Lynn looked at her with surprise. "What is it?"

"Well, there's skating, you know. Every day that the ice is good, there's a skating crowd in the park. It's not just for debutantes, it's for everybody. And there are school parties and dances for everybody, too. And the school clubs, except for a few that have somehow been taken over by the Hill crowd, are for everybody. There's no reason for dropping out of everything, just because you're not a debutante."

Lynn's eyes flashed. "That's a different song from the one you were singing a few months ago, when the debutante invitations first came out. Seems to me you were saying then that a girl who wasn't a debutante would be out of everything."

"I know," Dodie admitted. "I did feel like that then. But that was before I met Ronnie, before I got to know there were people who weren't from the Hill and were still worth knowing. Why, there's a whole world going on that's not connected with the Hill."

It seemed so funny to be lectured on snobbery by Dodie that Lynn was more amused than angry.

"O.K.," she said. "Maybe you're right. Maybe I got off on the wrong track."

After Dodie left, Lynn went back to her room and picked up her book again. She spent the rest of the after-noon reading—and thinking.

The last week of Christmas vacation passed slowly. When the evening of the debutante fashion show arrived, Lynn deposited herself in front of the television set.

Ernie paused, on his way through the living room. "Why don't you ride over with me?" he said. "It's the sort of thing I'd think you'd get a kick out of."

"You mean *you're* going?" Lynn stared at him in amaze-ment 'To a fashion show? I don't believe it!"

Ernie flushed. "Well, not for the show itself, of course. A lot I care about new spring dresses! But Nancy's model-ing, and she'd be pretty disappointed if I didn't turn up in the audience. Why don't you come with me?"

Lynn was tempted. She hesitated, and then suddenly she thought about the way it would be afterward. Ernie would be taking Nancy somewhere, probably to a drive-in for a ham-burger and coffee, and there would be others going. Perhaps even Paul. Paul with Brenda. And she, Lynn, would be the extra one.

She shook her head. "No, Ernie. Thanks anyway. There's good television tonight. I'd rather stay home."

Ernie shrugged his shoulders. "Suit yourself. I think you're being pretty silly."

He said the same thing at breakfast the next morning. "You missed a good show last night. You were silly not to go. You'd have had a good time."

"Were there a lot of people?" Lynn asked, curious in spite of herself.

"Mobs. They had it in the auditorium, and the place was jammed—never saw such a crowd. And at two dollars apiece, too. The debs must really have cleaned up."

"That means there'll be a good donation for the hospital." Lynn glanced sideways at her father, to see his reaction to this statement.

He merely nodded. Then he caught her looking at him, and his eyes began to twinkle.

"Look, kids," he said gruffly, "I know what's going on in this town. I'm perfectly aware of why Mrs. Peterson is being so darned generous to the hospital, and if you think I'm going to make any fuss about accepting that check, you're crazy. The hospital needs the money, and we're not turning down any legitimate donation that comes along. But if you think Mrs. Peterson is buying me off, you're equally crazy. I don't approve of debutantes—I never have, and I never will—and I'm sticking by that statement, no matter how many fashion shows she throws."

Mrs. Chambers said, "Your father is stubborn as an ox, children." But she was smiling, and Lynn could see that she was proud.

Suddenly, Lynn felt proud, too. She paused to give her father a quick kiss as she left the table.

"Good for you. Daddy!" she whispered.

Mrs. Chambers followed her into the hall. "Lynn, are you sure you feel well enough to start school today?" she asked anxiously. "You did have such a nasty bout of flu, and you seemed to feel so miserable over the holidays. If you want to stay home a few more days—"

"No, Mother," Lynn said, "I don't. I really feel fine."

"You're sure—" her mother said doubtfully.

"Yes, of course, I'm sure." Lynn pulled on her heavy coat and quickly tied a scarf over her head. "Come on, Dodie— we don't want to be late the very first day after the holidays!"

Ernie appeared in the doorway. "Well, I'll say good-by to you gals now, then. I'll probably be gone by the time you get home this afternoon."

"Oh," Lynn exclaimed, "are you going back today? I didn't think you had to leave until tomorrow!"

"With the roads the way they are, we thought we'd allow ourselves some extra time." Ernie gave her shoulder a pat. "Take care of yourself, Sis."

"You too, Ernie. Drive carefully."

"I will," Ernie promised. "And Paul's a careful driver, you know that."

"I know," Lynn said.

She thought, after driving around in Paul's car for over a year, I should know. I know how he drives, and how he looks when he drives—leaning forward a little over the wheel, concentrating on the road—and the way he doesn't like to talk much when he's driving, but he does like to play the radio very low—

The memories came flooding back, faster than she could shove them from her.

And now he's going, she thought—today—driving back to college! All along there's been a chance he might come by, a chance he might call—but not any more. After today, he'll be gone.

"Come on, Dodie," she called hoarsely, turning toward the door. "Let's get going, or we'll be late!"

Once outside, they walked in silence. The day was crisp and chilly, and their breath was steam in the cold air. They were halfway to school before Dodie spoke, and when she did, it was not in reference to Paul.

"Are you going to return Dirk's necklace today?"

Lynn nodded. "I have it in my coat pocket."

Until now, she had been dreading the ordeal of returning the necklace, but now she let herself think about it, glad to have something other than Paul to focus her mind upon.

"I thought I'd just hand it to him in the hall," she said, "or maybe at lunch time. I know if I try to talk to him, it will just be unpleasant."

Dodie nodded in agreement, and they walked on in companionable silence, which was broken only when they ran into Nancy and Joan at the curve in the road and joined forces with them the rest of the way.

They were not late for classes, but they were not early either, and there was little time for hanging around the halls and chatting with friends. The school was buzzing with after-Christmas chatter—"Wasn't the deb party at the Yacht Club the coolest thing you've ever been to?"— "Honestly, I've never been so embarrassed in my life. Here I had this dollar necktie for him, and then he came in with a handbag that must have cost fifteen dollars, at the very least!"—"Were you at the debutante fashion show? Did you ever see anything lovelier than that last gown Holly Taylor modeled?"

Lynn drifted through the halls in the direction of home room, hearing the talk around her but not really listening to it. She looked for Dirk as she walked, but she did not see him. She hesitated by his locker, thinking he might come there for his books, but when the warning bell rang, he still had not arrived.

Maybe he's gone on to his home room and is going to pick up his books before the first class, she thought.

She turned and continued down the hall to her own home room, arriving just as the final bell rang. Hastily, she slipped into her seat.

When the bell rang at the end of the period, Lynn left the room quickly and, after pausing briefly at her own locker, headed for Dirk's. This time, she was sure she saw him and that he saw her, but he was at the far end of the hall, and by the time she reached the place, he had lost himself in the crowd. Walking back the full length of the hall again, she was late entering English class.

Mrs. Mayor, the English teacher, gave her an odd look. "This is your first time late, Lynn, or I would have you go down to the attendance office for a tardy slip," she commented.

"I'm sorry," Lynn said, feeling her face grow red beneath the curious eyes which turned upon her.

"All right," Mrs. Mayor said kindly. "But let's not let it happen again."

Lynn usually enjoyed Mrs. Mayor's English class, but

today she could not concentrate on anything that was being said.

He's avoiding me, she thought, deliberately avoiding me. Of all the silly ways to act! Maybe he's mad at me, but that doesn't mean he has to go out of his way to be horrid. I'm going to feel like a perfect fool, looking all over the school for him when he doesn't want to be found. And it's not as though I want to talk to him—I just want to hand him the necklace.

When the bell rang at the end of the class, she got quickly to her feet and started toward the door, but this time she was delayed by Holly Taylor, who caught her arm as she went by.

"Hi, Lynn, where are you going in such a hurry? Stop and say hello!"

Lynn paused, unable to avoid answering the friendly greeting. Holly was one of the little knot of girls standing by the doorway. Nancy was with her, and so was Brenda Peterson.

"Hello," Lynn said politely. "What's new with the debutantes?"

"We missed you last night at the fashion show," Nancy told her. "Ernie said he tried to get you to go and couldn't talk you into it. I wish you had come; it was lots of fun."

"And we made a fortune," Brenda added. "Over five hundred dollars! I'm taking it over to the hospital this afternoon. I meant to drop it off on the way to school, but I got delayed and didn't have time to make it."

"Five hundred dollars is a lot of money to tote around high school all day," Lynn remarked. It gave her a feeling of satisfaction to place Brenda in the wrong. "Something might happen to it."

"Oh, I'm not that silly," Brenda said. "Mother let me drive the car to school this morning, and I locked my wallet inside. In fact," she gave a helpless little smile that irritated Lynn immeasurably, "I guess I locked my own money up at the same time. I'm going to have to make a trip out to the parking lot, if I want lunch today."

Nancy said, "You're headed for Spanish, aren't you, Lynn? I'll walk you over."

As they went down the hall, Lynn caught a glimpse of Dirk again, standing near his locker, but she could not break away from her friend and go rushing after him. She had still not had a chance to hand him the necklace when the next bell rang.

This is getting ridiculous, Lynn thought, as she seated herself in Spanish class and waited for the day's assignment to be given. Then she caught sight of Anne. She was sitting quietly in her usual seat in the corner, hemmed in by her friends, Clara and Rachel.

Anne, Lynn thought. Why didn't I think of her before? She'll be able to find Dirk for me; surely she knows his schedule, and he won't be avoiding *her*.

She hesitated and then, for the first time in her life, opened her notebook and tore out a clean piece of paper and wrote a few quick lines. She folded the paper quickly and, when no one was looking, tossed it neatly across the row of desks between hers and Anne's.

The note fell with a little plop on to Anne's Spanish book.

Anne glanced up in surprise. Her eyes skipped over

the room until they met Lynn's. She raised her eyebrows questioningly. Lynn nodded. Quickly, under cover of her notebook, Anne opened the note, scanned it hurriedly and glanced up again. Again her eyes met Lynn's, and this time she shook her head.

Lynn stared at her in bewilderment. The note had read, "I must see Dirk as soon as possible. Where can I find him?" What was there in that to shake your head about?

She motioned to Anne to write a return note, but again Anne shook her head and made a slight gesture toward the clock. Lynn followed her gaze and saw that there were only ten minutes left before the class would be over. There was hardly sense in exchanging notes again now; the risk was not worth it.

The ten minutes seemed to drag on endlessly. When the bell finally rang, however, it was Anne who slipped quickly from her seat and crossed to Lynn's desk.

"Do you really have to see Dirk?" she asked in a low voice when she reached it. "Isn't it anything I can say to him for you?"

"You mean he's *that* angry!" Lynn exclaimed in horror. "Oh, Anne!"

"I've never seen him so upset about anything," Anne said quietly. "I was sitting in the living room the day he phoned you, so I couldn't help but hear part of it. I don't know exactly what it was you told him, or why, but when he hung up that telephone, he looked as though someone had kicked him. What was it all about?"

"I told him I wasn't going to date him," Lynn said, hating to see the hurt in Anne's eyes. "It's not that I don't like him, Anne, and last time he was awfully sweet to me. It's just that he was getting too serious. And I could never care about him the way he seemed to be getting to care about me. It seemed better to break off completely than to drag it on and have him care more."

Anne digested this, then nodded slowly in agreement "Yes, you're right if that's the way it was. But do you have to go talk to him now? He's so hurt and angry, it couldn't do anything but make it worse."

Lynn considered briefly handing the necklace to Anne and asking her to give it to Dirk, but her conscience would not let her do that. After all, she thought, he gave it to me himself, and Anne knows nothing about it. Probably he doesn't want her to know anything about it either—especially now.

She shook her head. "I *do* have to see him. There's no getting around that. It will just take a minute, but I do have to see him myself."

"All right," Anne said. "If you have to." She glanced at the clock on the wall. "You probably just have time to catch him, if you hurry. Brad Morgan called as we were leaving for school this morning. He said there's something wrong with his car and he wants Dirk to look at it. He said he'd stop and pick him up at lunch hour. I kind of got the impression Dirk was going to cut classes the rest of the day and not come back to school at all."

Lynn said, "Then he'd be in the parking lot?"

"I suppose so," Anne said, "unless they've left already." Which was how Lynn came to be running across the parking lot at just the moment to hear Brenda Peterson, her voice shaking with fury, cry, "It's gone! The whole five hundred dollars—it's gone! Those terrible boys have taken it!"

12

"What do you mean, we've taken it?" Lynn heard Dirk's voice before she actually saw him. "What five hundred dollars? What the dickens are you talking about, anyway?"

"You know perfectly well what I'm talking about," Brenda returned angrily. "The more than five hundred dollars that was in my wallet, right here in the front seat of my mother's car. Now the door's open and the wallet's gone!"

Hurrying around the side of the Peterson car, Lynn came face to face with the three of them—Brenda, her usually pale face flushed with anger, Dirk and Brad Morgan. Dirk, standing with his hands in his pockets, was the picture of outrage. Brad merely looked amused.

"Well, hi, there!" he said lightly as Lynn came into view. "This little friend of yours seems to be blowing her top about something. Can you make out what it's all about?"

Lynn's first impulse was to be amused also, for Brenda and Dirk looked so furious, standing there glaring at each other. But as soon as the meaning of the scene began to penetrate, the amusement changed to horror.

"You mean the hospital money, Brenda? The hospital money's gone?"

"Yes, it's gone!" Brenda turned the storm of her wrath toward Lynn. "And I know where it's gone, too—right into their pockets. They were standing here by the car when I came up. It couldn't have been anyone else."

"But how," Lynn asked in bewilderment, "could the door have been opened? I thought you said you locked it."

"I did," Brenda answered bitterly. "I must not have caught the latch at the wing window. It's been forced, and when I got here, the car door was standing wide open."

"Well, we didn't have a thing to do with it!" Dirk said angrily. "I got here just about two seconds before you did. You're not going to blame this thing on me!"

Their voices carried across the parking lot, and a crowd was beginning to gather. A group of girls who had started toward their car paused instead to listen to the argument. Several younger boys, who had been playing football in the schoolyard, broke into a run at the sound of possible trouble. They came panting up, eagerly throwing themselves into the conversation.

"What happened? What's the matter? Who did what anyway?"

"These two boys," Brenda repeated for the benefit of her new audience, "they broke into my car and took my wallet."

"That's a pretty strong thing to assert," a masculine voice said firmly. "Do you have any proof to back up your accusation, young lady?"

Lynn turned in relief to see Mr. Ryan, the football coach and boys' physical education teacher. His quiet voice cut through the turmoil, stilling the excitement as though by magic.

Brenda said, "Look in their pockets. That should be proof. You don't find many high-school boys carrying five hundred dollars around in their pockets."

"No," Mr. Ryan agreed, "that's true enough. All right boys, just to clear this thing up, let's see what you have in your pockets."

Brad hesitated a moment, then shrugged and pulled his pockets inside out. A jumble of articles tumbled onto the ground—a pocketknife, a package of cigarettes, some assorted coins, car keys, a packet of matches, a soiled pocket handkerchief. Mr. Ryan gave the objects a quick glance and then motioned the young man to pick them up.

"Can't find five hundred there, by any stretch of the imagination. O.K., Masters, you're next. Pockets out!" Mr. Ryan said.

"I will not turn my pockets out!" Dirk's face was dark with fury. "This is the rottenest thing I've ever heard of! I didn't have a thing to do with her darned car—it was standing here with the door hanging open when I came up, and she came screaming around the comer two seconds later. Nobody's going to go rooting through my things— not unless they go to the police station and get a search warrant!"

"Don't make us do that, Son." There was an edge to Mr. Ryan's voice now. "If you're innocent, there's no sense in making a scene about this thing. Turn out your pockets."

Dirk's head was thrown back, his dark eyes were blazing. "Let's see you make me!"

Moved in spite of herself by the boy's defiance, Lynn had an urge to walk over and stand beside him. No wonder he's angry, she thought. I know how I'd feel if somebody told *me* to turn everything out of my pocketbook to prove I wasn't a thief. I'd be so mad I'd probably throw it at them.

But at that instant, Brad Morgan spoke, his voice low and scornful.

"Oh, come on, Dirk, give them their way. There's no sense making a big thing out of it."

Dirk hesitated and then, with a look of disgust, emptied his pockets onto the ground.

In the silence that followed, Brenda said, "What about his gym bag? Open that, too. Maybe he has it in his gym bag."

Dirk's gym bag was on the ground at his feet. Now he gave it a savage kick in Brenda's direction.

"Sure," he said bitterly, "better examine everything. Better play safe and open it yourselves, too—I might have a gun in there and shoot all your heads off."

Mr. Ryan said, "O.K., Son, calm down. This will just take a minute."

He lifted the gym bag and pulled out a pair of gym shoes, some tennis shorts—and a pale pink, lady's wallet.

"That's it!" Brenda exclaimed. "That's the wallet! Is the money still in it?"

Mr. Ryan was regarding the wallet with surprise. Slowly, he opened it and looked inside.

"Yes," he said quietly, "there's money here. A lot of money." He ruffled through it quickly. "There's more than five hundred dollars here. Five hundred and a little extra."

"We made over five hundred and I had a few dollars of my own there, too." Brenda explained, reaching for the money. "Could I have it please?"

"Yes," Mr. Ryan said "I suppose so." He handed the wallet to Brenda and then turned his attention to Dirk. "Well, young man, what do you have to say for yourself?"

Dirk was staring at the wallet in bewilderment. "Nothing," he said. "That is, I don't know anything about it. I didn't put it in my gym bag. I never saw it before in my life." He looked very young, and suddenly scared. "Honest, I didn't have anything to do with it."

"Now look, Masters," Mr. Ryan said patiently, "you can't expect anybody to believe that."

"I believe him!" Lynn said suddenly. "Dirk didn't take that wallet! He wouldn't do a thing like that!"

She did not know how she knew, she just knew. The certainty in her voice swung everyone's attention in her direction.

"How—" Mr. Ryan began.

But Brenda interrupted him. "Of course, Lynn Chambers is going to stick up for him! Lynn and Dirk have been going together all through Christmas vacation. In fact, I just mentioned to Lynn this morning that I had left the money locked in the car. I wouldn't be a bit surprised if she told Dirk about it herself!"

When she thought about it afterward, during the long, wretched time afterward, it was that moment that Lynn remembered. Not the time in the principal's office waiting for her parents and Mrs. Peterson to arrive, not the interview itself, with her mother's pale face on one side of her and Mrs. Peterson's outraged one on the other, but that first unbelievable moment when Brenda had faced her in front of the whole crowd of people and said, "She told Dirk about it herself!"

"Why, that's not true!" Lynn had gasped in horror. "It's not true at all! What a perfectly terrible thing to say!"

"Brenda!" Nancy's voice broke into the conversation,

equally horrified. "Brenda, that's *Lynn* you're talking to! How can you say such a thing?"

There was a rustle in the crowd as a slender, red-haired girl pushed her way forward until she was by her friend's side. "Brenda's upset, Lynn. She can't mean it—"

"I do mean it!" Brenda said. "I did tell Lynn just this morning. You were there, Nancy—you heard me yourself—"

"All right, all right," Mr. Ryan cut in quickly, evidently feeling he had let the scene drag on far enough. "This isn't the time or place to go into this. There are only four people involved, and I want them to come with me to the principal's office. The rest of you move along. Your lunch hour's half over already, and if you don't get over to the cafeteria in a hurry, you're going to be pretty hungry the rest of the day."

Amid much muttering and glancing at watches, the crowd began to drift away.

Brad spoke for the first time since he had advised Dirk to empty his pockets. "I don't have to come, do I? I don't have a thing to do with this—I'm not even a student here. I was just a bystander, and I've got a date somewhere else in about five minutes."

Mr. Ryan hesitated. "Well—"

"Thanks." Brad threw Lynn an amused glance and gave Dirk's shoulder a pat of encouragement. "Good luck, Masters. Hope everything turns out O.K. for you!"

He walked over to his car, got in, and started the engine.

"Are you going to let him go?" Lynn asked, as the car pulled out of the parking lot. "He was in on everything, just as much as Dirk was."

"But he didn't have a gym bag with the wallet in it," Mr.

Ryan reminded her quietly. "Come on, you three—let's go over to the principal's office and see if we can't get this thing straightened out."

The next few hours always seemed to Lynn like a nightmare—an odd, distorted nightmare, with everyone in the wrong places doing the wrong things. Several times before she had been in the principal's office on class business and noticed students sitting miserably on the long benches along the back wall, waiting to be interviewed about misconduct. She had always regarded them with a kind of pitying scorn—they were the students who were caught smoking or playing hookey or writing words on the washroom mirrors. They had no connection with Lynn or with the Hill crowd, and she seldom knew their names or saw them again.

And now, Lynn thought, I'm one of those students!

She seated herself with as much dignity as possible on the end of the bench.

Mr. Ryan spoke for a few moments with Mr. Curtis, the principal. Then the two men walked over to the bench.

"This is serious business," Mr. Curtis said quietly. "I don't want to go into it until your parents are here. Can you tell me where I can reach them?"

Brenda answered quickly, giving her address and telephone number. Lynn did the same.

Dirk looked defiant. "My dad's working."

"We want to call him, anyway," Mr. Curtis said. "I'm sure he can get off from work for a little while for something as important as this."

"He won't," Dirk said bitterly. "He doesn't give a darn about what I do." But after a moment, he gave the name and telephone number of Hendricks' Grocery Store, where his father worked in the afternoons.

It was only a matter of about twenty minutes before Mrs. Chambers arrived, and an instant later Dr. Chambers himself strode in. He shook hands with Mr. Ryan and spoke to Mr. Curtis, whom he knew from Rotary.

"What is this ridiculous thing, Clint?" he asked briskly "Are you actually accusing my daughter of being mixed up in a robbery?"

"Of course not, Nathan," Mr. Curtis said easily. "She just happened to be on the scene when this thing happened, and I thought you would want to be in on it while we got it straightened out."

"Well, good—I'm glad you called me." Mollified, Dr. Chambers walked over to the bench and seated herself on one side of Lynn. Mrs. Chambers was already on Lynn's other side, talking to her softly.

A few moments later, Mrs. Peterson rushed into the room, chattering excitedly. She flew to her daughter's side and put her arm around her. "Brenda, baby!" she breathed dramatically. "Are you all right?"

"Of course, I'm all right," Brenda told her. "It's the hospital money that—"

At that moment the door opened again, and another man walked in. It was Mr. Masters. He came slowly into the room, moving heavily. His weathered face was lined with worry. He glanced at the group of people before him, nodded briefly at Lynn, and then his eyes settled upon Dirk. Without a word, he went over and sat down beside him.

"Dad—" Dirk looked up in amazement. "I didn't think you'd come!"

"Not come? I'm your father, aren't I?" Mr. Masters turned his gaze upon Mr. Curtis. "What is this all about?"

It did not take long to go over the story. Brenda told about leaving the wallet locked in the car and about coming back to the parking lot to get her lunch money and finding the car door standing open.

"The wing window was forced open," she said, "and the wallet was gone, and Dirk here and another fellow were just starting away from it. I insisted that they be searched, and Dirk had the wallet in his gym bag."

"But I didn't take it!" Dirk insisted. "I don't know how it got there, but I didn't take it. I went out to the parking lot to meet my friend, Brad Morgan. He was picking me up to help do some work on his car. He was there when I got there—we talked a few minutes and then started to walk over to where his car was parked. Now I think back on it, I remember the door of the Peterson car was standing open, but I hardly noticed it at the time."

"But you had the wallet!" Brenda exclaimed. "And Lynn could have told you it was in the car—I mentioned it to her myself this morning—"

"That's an absurd accusation," Dr. Chambers broke in angrily. "Lynn wouldn't have anything to do with stealing anything. You carelessly left a wallet lying on the front seat of your car. Anybody looking in the car window would have seen it there. Nobody had to be informed about it."

"But Lynn *could* have told him." Brenda turned to her mother. "Lynn never has liked me, Mother, especially since I became a debutante and started going around with her old crowd. And she knew that I was responsible for the money and would be in trouble if anything happened to it." She turned back to Lynn. "I don't think you would ever actually break into a car and take something, but I do think you could have told Dirk about it. Why, the way you stuck up for him out there on the parking lot proves you have some connection with it. You can't think he is innocent!"

Staring back into Brenda's cold blue eyes, Lynn's anger was tempered with astonishment . . . Why, she actually believes what she is saying! She isn't just trying to get me in trouble—she actually believes it!

But all she could think of to say was, "I do think Dirk is innocent. I don't just think it—I *know* it."

"And I know it, too." Mr. Masters' deep voice rang out strongly through the small room "My son may have done some foolish things in his young life, but he is not a thief. And he is not a liar. If he says he doesn't know how that wallet got in his bag, then he doesn't know."

In the silence that followed these words, Dr. Chambers got quietly to his feet. "Whatever you decide here, Clint, I don't think it involves us. I've probably got an office full of patients waiting for me by this time. If it's all right with you, I'm going to take my wife and daughter home and get back to work."

Mr. Curtis nodded in agreement. "All right Nathan. Thanks for coming down. I appreciate it."

"I appreciate your calling me. Good afternoon, Brenda—Mrs. Peterson." With one arm around his wife and the other around his daughter, Dr. Chambers swept them out of the office.

"He believed me," Lynn said afterward, in the car on the way home. "I said I didn't have anything to do with the robbery, and Mr. Curtis believed me."

"Of course, he believed you," her father said.

"But he didn't believe Dirk. Dirk said he was innocent too."

"Dirk had the wallet," her mother reminded her gently.

"Even so—" Lynn tried to put her thoughts into words. "If the wallet had been in *my* bag, and I had said I didn't know how it got there, they would have thought twice about it, wouldn't they? Because I'm Lynn Chambers, because you are Dr. Nathan Chambers, and we live on the Hill? It would have made a difference, wouldn't it? I mean, they would have listened to me when I said I didn't put the wallet in the bag, and they would have tried to figure out some other way it could have got there, instead of just taking it for granted that I had stolen it."

"Yes," Dr. Chambers said quietly, "they probably would have."

When Dodie came home from school that afternoon, no one had to tell her about the robbery, she was bursting with excitement about it already.

"It's all over school!" she exclaimed. "Dirk Masters has been expelled. Mrs. Peterson is being surprisingly decent about it, though. She says that, since she has the money back, she isn't going to have the police called in."

"That *is* sweet of her," Lynn remarked caustically. Then she said, "Dirk didn't take that wallet, Dodie."

Her sister looked surprised. "What makes you think he didn't? They found it in his gym bag."

"I don't care where they found it; he didn't take it. You should have seen his face when they opened that bag and the wallet fell out! Why, he was just as surprised as anyone

else. He looked as though he couldn't believe it."

"They must be pretty sure," Dodie said, "if he's been expelled." She frowned. "There's some other talk too, Lynn. It sounds crazy, but somebody told me that Brenda was trying to drag you into it."

"She was," Lynn said. "But she couldn't do it."

"Imagine!" Dodie exclaimed angrily. "How could she have the nerve? Aren't you furious?"

"No," Lynn said slowly, surprised at her own words, "I'm not. That's funny, isn't it, considering how I've always felt about her? But I'm not. I think she actually believed what she said. And—and I kind of respect her for coming out and saying it, with me right there and Daddy and Mother standing behind me. I never thought she had it in her to do something like that."

"Well, *I* don't respect her," Dodie said decidedly. "I think she's horrid. And I'd keep an eye on her, Lynn. Just because she wasn't able to convince Mr. Curtis, don't be so sure she is simply going to let the whole thing drop."

"Oh, don't be silly!" Lynn exclaimed irritably, wishing Dodie's tongue were not quite so pointed. "I'm sick of talking about the whole thing. Let's drop it and forget about it."

She was to remember her sister's words, however. The next morning, when she got to school, the Hill crowd was assembled in its usual place, just left of the front steps. They were talking when Lynn first saw them. All of them seemed to be talking at once, in the way they had when they were discussing something exciting.

Lynn quickened her pace, but as she reached them, the talk seemed suddenly to die away.

Someone said, "Hi, Lynn!"

It was the signal for everyone to turn toward her. Silence hung heavy and strained over them, an odd, uncomfortable silence for which there seemed no reason.

"It wasn't the way it is when they're all discussing the debutante parties, and I come up," Lynn explained to Dodie later. "That has happened lots of times, and they just say 'hi' and go right ahead. I was sort of on the edge of the group, but I was not shut out of it, if you know what I mean." She hesitated, trying to keep the hurt from showing too much in her voice. "It was as though they were talking about *me*—as though they were in the middle of saying something about me, and I walked in on it, and—and—"

She stopped, not knowing how to describe it. Finally she continued, "I felt as though I ought to say 'excuse me' and turn around and walk away."

Dodie nodded slowly. There was no surprise in her voice when she said, "I can imagine." Then she asked, "Was Brenda in the group?"

"Yes," Lynn said, "she was."

As she spoke the words, she visualized the group again; and she felt a sudden wave of understanding, a horrible, dragging wave of understanding, mixed with despair.

"Yes," she repeated, "she was. Brenda was in the group. In fact, she was in the very middle of it."

13

It was a long time until spring.

It was odd, Lynn thought, how quickly spring seemed to come other years. The second semester always passed much more quickly than the first—there were skating parties and the Valentine Hop and tryouts for the spring play, and all the general "we're-in-the-home-stretch" feeling that came with the second half of the school year. One day it was January, the deepest part of winter, and the very next morning, it seemed, you turned around and there it was—spring.

This year, however, the days crept by slowly—January and January and more January, and when February finally arrived and began its own long, dragging process, spring seemed as far away as before.

"I've never been through such a long winter in my whole life," Lynn said miserably to Nancy. "Everybody treats me like I had a disease or something. What's the matter with them, Nan? What on earth did Brenda tell them?"

"She didn't exactly *tell* them anything," Nancy said slowly-

The two girls were walking home from school together. They were together a lot now; it was as though Nancy were trying as much as possible to make up to Lynn for the strained atmosphere she experienced with the others.

"She didn't tell anything," she repeated, "it was more that she hinted. She just sort of said, 'Isn't it odd the way Lynn turned up almost as soon as the robbery was committed, especially since I had just told her that morning about leaving my wallet in the car—and the way she stood up for Dirk and said he didn't have anything to do with it, when he had the money right there in his gym bag? Of course, she never liked me anyway, and she dated Dirk all during Christmas vacation'—oh, you know how she could say it."

"And they all listened to her," Lynn said bitterly. "All the people I thought were my friends. They think I told Dirk about the wallet and then lied for him by saying he didn't take it."

"Well, you *did* go out with Dirk," Nancy said helplessly, "not just once, but a couple of times. And everyone knows you don't like Brenda. *I* know you weren't involved in this thing, Lynn, and so do your other friends—your real friends. But it's actually not so farfetched that you can blame other people who don't know you so well for wondering."

"Yes, they're wondering, all right," Lynn said. "I can feel that wonder as thick as a fog wherever I go. I didn't get asked to the Valentine Hop; I didn't get a part in the spring play; I didn't even get elected to the honor club this semester, even though I had one of the highest averages in the class. And the worst part is, Nan, that it isn't just the people who don't know me. It's girls I've known and gone around with for years."

The hurt was sharp in her voice. Just the day before, she had come into the cafeteria late and carried her tray over to her usual table and sat down beside Joan Wilson. A few moments later, Joan had risen to get dessert, and when she returned, it was to sit at another table.

Lynn had tried to eat after that, but the food had tasted like meal in her mouth. After a few bites, she had left the table herself, and when she looked back, she saw Joan returning to seat herself in her old place.

Not that there weren't some friendly people left in the class. It was odd which ones they were. Nancy, of course, was still her closest friend, closer than ever, now that the other friends were fewer. Holly Taylor and several of the other Hill girls seemed to go out of their way to be friendly, as though to try to make up for the others. Anne's friends, Rachel Goldman and Clara Marivella, always spoke pleasantly, and once or twice asked Lynn if she wanted to go to a movie with them or stop at their homes in the afternoon to do homework.

"I suppose it's even harder," Lynn said thoughtfully, "for Anne than for me. After all, Dirk is her brother."

Nancy looked uncomfortable. "That's another thing," she said, "the way you are seeing so much of Anne. You're with her all the time these days."

"I like her," Lynn asserted shortly. "I thought you liked her, too. You said so at the beginning of the year."

"I know I did," Nancy agreed. "And I still like her. But I don't think you're smart to be seen with her so constantly. She's Dirk's sister, and if you seem to be awfully friendly with her, people are naturally going to think you are with Dirk, too. And that can't do anything but make the situation worse."

"I like Anne," Lynn said stubbornly. "And I like Dirk.

And I don't believe he did this thing. But you think he did, don't you, Nan?"

"Yes," Nancy answered truthfully, "I think he probably did. But I believe that *you* don't think he did, and that's what matters." She slipped her arm through Lynn's. "I have a good idea. Why don't you come over tonight and hear my new batch of records? I bet you haven't even heard the one you gave me yourself for Christmas. And we could try our luck with home permanents and really make kind of a 'hen evening' of it, the way we used to."

"Tonight?" Lynn looked surprised. "Isn't tonight the debutantes' Valentine party? I thought they were going to have it a week early, to keep it from coinciding with the school's Valentine Hop."

"No," Nancy said, "the school is having theirs early, so it won't get in the way of the debutantes'. Not that it would matter, because the debutantes aren't planning to bother with the Hop, and most of the boys don't want to go to two Valentine parties in a row, so nobody will be at the school dance, anyway." She shook her head. "And it's a shame, because those school dances used to be lots of fun."

"They certainly did," Lynn said, remembering the dances she and Paul had been to the year before. And with the thought of Paul, a whole raft of memories flooded over her—Paul wearing a tuxedo and a much-too-short haircut, awkwardly handing her a box with her first corsage in it. Paul dancing the way only Paul danced, with that smooth dip after each turn which made dancing seem more like flying. Paul holding her hand as they walked away from the gym afterward, with music still floating soft and sweet in the night behind them, and the feel of his hand, hard and warm, around her own, the expression on his face when he turned to look down at her.

Lynn gave her head a little shake to make the memories go away, but they clung, and her throat tightened, and she felt the sting of tears in her eyes.

"Not tonight," she said quickly to Nancy. "Thanks anyway, but I don't think I can come over tonight. Another time, maybe." And she turned away.

Her parents did not know about the cloud hanging over her. They knew something was wrong. They knew her well enough to see that she was not happy, and she realized that they worried about her, but she could not bring herself to tell them what the matter was. Mrs. Chambers thought she was brooding about Paul, and Dr. Chambers was sure it was a general letdown following the flu, and he kept plying her with vitamins and iron pills.

Of course, Dodie knew, but she was not too sympathetic. "The way you stood up for Dirk," she said, "you really brought the whole thing on yourself. Why do you have to keep saying he didn't do it when everyone knows he did?"

"But he *didn't*," Lynn insisted.

"Well, if he didn't," Dodie said impatiently, "who did? The wallet was taken—you can't deny that. Somebody took it out of Brenda's car and put it in Dirk's gym bag. Who did it? And why?"

Lynn was startled. For all her insistence on Dirk's innocence, she had not once carried the question far enough to ask herself who was guilty. But now, hearing it put into words, the question sprang clear and sharp to the front of her mind, as though she had been thinking about it constantly.

And, just as suddenly, she had an answer. "Brad!"

"Brad?" Dodie looked at her in surprise. "Brad who?"

"Brad Morgan."

"Who on earth is Brad Morgan?" Dodie asked in bewilderment. "I haven't heard anybody mention him in connection with the robbery."

"But he was there," Lynn said. "Right there, all the while things were going on. And then he left. He never offered to stay with Dirk or gave him any support; he just walked out. And he was supposed to be Dirk's friend."

"But why," Dodie asked, "would he put the wallet in Dirk's gym bag? That seems like a crazy thing to do. And why wouldn't Dirk have seen him do it?"

"I don't know," Lynn said slowly. "I don't know. But I'm going to find out."

Now that she had a definite project in mind, Lynn suddenly found the whole situation less depressing. She went to bed that night and, for the first time in weeks, slept soundly and contentedly.

The first thing Lynn did when she got to school the next morning was to look for Anne. "Where," she asked, drawing her into a corner, "can I find Dirk?"

"Dirk?" Anne looked surprised. "Why, at work, I guess. He has a full-time job at Burton's Garage. Dad knows the man who runs it, and he talked him into taking Dirk on, even though he was expelled."

"Is that the garage on 40th Street?"

Anne nodded. "You know, it's funny, but Dirk's been like a new person since he was expelled from school. He's angry about it, of course—at the school and at Brenda and

Mrs. Peterson—but he's not angry at *himself*. He holds his head up and looks you in the eye and says, 'I'm not a thief and nobody's going to turn me into one, just by saying I am.' It's a way Dirk has never acted before. And he's changed with Dad."

"He looked so surprised to see his father at school that day," Lynn said. "He never expected him to come."

"Dad's been wonderful," Anne said. "He's never once questioned Dirk about anything. In fact, when Dirk tried to tell him he hadn't done it, Dad just said, 'I know you didn't, Son,' and changed the subject. And he is so proud of Dirk's job at the garage. He calls him 'a working man' and acts as if Dirk quit school because he wanted to, not because he had to."

Lynn said, "I want to see Dirk. I want to talk to him."

Anne looked troubled. "Must you, Lynn? Things have worked themselves out pretty well for us, considering. It's hard, of course, but your seeing him couldn't make it any easier. All it could do would be to stir things up all over again. Wouldn't it be better just to let it rest?"

"No," Lynn answered decidedly. "What I have to see Dirk about is important. I think he'll want to talk to me when he learns what it is."

The next afternoon, after school, instead of walking home along the River Road and up the Hill, Lynn caught a bus toward town and got off at Burton's Garage.

A mechanic in coveralls was sprawled on the ground, half under an automobile, doing something to it with a wrench.

"Hello," Lynn said tentatively. "Can you tell me where

I can find Dirk Masters?"

The mechanic turned and looked up at her, and Lynn caught her breath sharply at the sight of the thin, dark face and the familiar shock of dark hair curling forward over the forehead.

She exclaimed, "Oh! Oh, I didn't recognize you in your work clothes."

Dirk's surprise was even greater than hers. He stared at her in silence for a moment. Then he asked, "What are you doing here?"

"I want to talk to you," Lynn answered awkwardly. Now that she was actually face to face with Dirk, she found she did not know exactly what to say to him. She had forgotten how terribly angry he had been with her the last time they had talked. Now she remembered, and the memory was not a pleasant one. She felt uncomfortable.

"Please," she urged.

Dirk asked, "What about? We don't have much to talk about, you and I."

"We *do* have something to talk about," Lynn contradicted him. "The robbery."

"I'm a working man now," Dirk said. "I don't get off till five o'clock."

"Then I'll wait."

"It's only three-thirty. You can't just stand here an hour and a half."

"There's a bench over there," Lynn said. "I'll go sit on it and wait for you. It will give me a chance to get some studying done."

The afternoon passed slowly. Lynn opened her Spanish book and went through the vocabulary, slowly repeating the words to herself. Every once in a while she would raise her eyes and glance around until she located Dirk. When he said, "I'm a working man," he had meant it, because he was indeed working, and hard. He finished the job he was doing when Lynn came in, and an older man, evidently his boss, joined him on the ground, to examine the car. A few moments later, he got up again and gave Dirk a good-natured whack on the shoulder. It was a man-to-man gesture, and Dirk straightened up and looked pleased and turned briskly to start work on another car.

Watching him, Lynn thought there was nothing defensive about him when he was like this, working at something he was interested in and being treated as an equal by other men. It made him seem almost like a man himself. In fact when five o'clock finally came, and Dirk slowly crossed over to her, she felt an odd shyness in his presence, as though she were going to have an interview with a stranger.

But as he reached her, the manliness slid aside, and it was the old, half-mocking voice that said, "Well, I didn't think you'd really stick it out and wait for me."

"I told you I would," Lynn said, getting up. "I want to talk to you."

"We can't talk here," Dirk said, "the place is closing. And I don't think you'd especially want to be seen around town with a greasy garage repairman."

"Of course, I don't mind being seen with you," Lynn said, her old irritation coming to life again. "Why do you always try to make me seem such a snob, Dirk?"

He did not answer. Instead, he nodded toward a car parked alongside the garage.

"Come on then. I'll drive you home."

Lynn rose and followed him over to the car. She climbed in beside him, her eyes wide with amazement.

"Is this really yours?"

"Yeah, it's mine." Dirk could not keep a touch of pride from his voice. "It may be kind of old, but it runs. My boss here got it on a trade-in. He and the other guys have been helping me fix it up, and I'm paying for it every month out of my salary."

Lynn said, "That's wonderful! And it's a fine car!" She hesitated and then asked slowly, "Now you don't have to borrow Brad's, do you?"

Dirk said, "I wouldn't be borrowing it anyway. Not after his walking out on me, back in the school parking lot, without saying a word to help me. And I thought he was my friend!" He gave a short laugh. "Some friend he turned out to be!"

Lynn said, "That's what I wanted to talk to you about." She paused, trying to think how to approach the subject. Then she turned, to find Dirk looking at her.

"About Brad?"

"Yes." Lynn drew a deep breath. "Dirk, did you ever think he might have taken the wallet himself?"

Dirk drove in silence for a moment. When he spoke, it was slowly. "I suppose he could have. He was there already, you know, when I came up. It wouldn't have been impossible. But it was in *my* gym bag!"

"Couldn't he have put it there?" Lynn asked. "Were you watching him—and it—the whole time?"

"I was talking with him," Dirk said. "I wanted to know what he thought was wrong with his car, before I started working on it. I asked him, and he said, 'Come on, let's go.

We'll go into that later.' Come to think of it, he was in an awful hurry to get out of there. And then that Peterson girl came around the corner and saw her car door open and gave a shriek like a fire siren, and I turned to see what was the matter with her—" He broke off the sentence and then repeated it, as though hearing himself for the first time. "I turned to see what was the matter! Right then, I wasn't looking at Brad at all!"

"And the gym bag?" Lynn asked eagerly. "Where was the gym bag?"

"On the ground, between Brad and me."

"Then that was it." Lynn relaxed against the back of the seat. "That was the moment. Brad had probably just taken the wallet when you came up to him; he could have seen it just from glancing in the window of the car. He wouldn't have had to know there was five hundred dollars in it in order to take it. Then, when Brenda arrived, he knew there was going to be a showdown. When you looked away, he slipped the wallet into your gym bag, so if you were searched, it would be found on you, instead of him."

Dirk was looking straight ahead, his eyes on the road. . . . He nodded slowly. "Yes, Princess, 1 think you've got it. That's the way it must have been."

They had been driving along the River Road. Now they came to the corner, and Dirk slowed and turned up the Hill and pulled to a stop in front of the Chambers' house.

He switched off the motor and leaned back, his eyes on Lynn. "Well," he said, "do you feel like Sherlock Holmes?"

"I certainly do!" Lynn smiled at him. "For goodness' sake, what's the matter? Aren't you happy we've worked it out?"

"Sure," Dirk answered. "I've been wondering how it could have happened the way it did. I'm glad to get it figured out. But I'm not just panting with joy. It's not like I could do anything about it."

"What do you mean?" Lynn asked in astonishment. "You can go to Mr. Curtis and tell him about Brad and how it all happened. Once it's all cleared up, you can come back to school again. You're a senior, Dirk; surely you want to graduate?"

"You mean, you think Mr. Curtis will believe me? You think all I have to do is go tell him that somebody else did it and he's going to say, 'I'm so glad to hear it now everything's all right?' Come down to earth, kid. I could go around yelling, 'Brad Morgan did it' from now to kingdom come, and nobody would listen to me—only Anne and my dad."

Lynn felt her happiness slipping away. "But if I went with you, too—if we went together—if *I* told them—"

Dirk was looking at her in an odd way. He asked, "You really believe it, don't you—that I didn't do it? You've believed it all along? You even said so to Mr. Curtis and the others."

"Yes." Lynn reached out impulsively and caught his hand. "Dirk, surely we can do *something!*"

Dirk shook his head. "No," he said quietly, "I don't think we can. But—but thanks, anyway." He leaned across her and opened the car door. "Hop out, Princess. You're home."

Lynn regarded him helplessly. "Then you're not going to Mr. Curtis at all?"

"What good would it do?" Suddenly, as Lynn started to get out of the car, he tightened his hand on hers. "Look—

you know on the telephone—when you said you wanted to be friends? Did you mean that?"

"Of course." Lynn said, a trifle impatiently. "Would I have come today if I hadn't?"

"I'm sorry," Dirk said, "about what I answered. I was mad, I guess, and hurt. Is—is it too late—to change my mind?"

"No," Lynn told him warmly, "it's not too late." She gave his hand a quick squeeze and slipped out of the car. "Good-by, Dirk."

"So long, Princess."

Mrs. Chambers was in the living room as Lynn entered. She looked up and smiled.

"Hello, darling. You're awfully late getting home from school. Was there a meeting or something?"

Lynn nodded vaguely. "I got involved. You know how it is."

"I'm glad," her mother said gently. "I've been worried about you this term. You haven't seemed to take any interest in school activities. Daddy and I were talking last night We wonder if maybe we didn't make a mistake by asking you not to be a debutante. Somehow, proving a point doesn't seem nearly so important if it means your daughter's unhappiness."

"No," Lynn said, admitting it for the first time, "you weren't wrong. Some of the finest girls in our class aren't debutantes, and I would probably never have met them if I had been one."

"Then maybe it has been worth while." Her mother's face suddenly brightened. "Oh, I almost forgot there's a letter for you. It's on the hall table."

"A letter?" Lynn was surprised. "I'm not expecting any letters."

She went into the hall. There, on the table, was an envelope. She picked it up and caught her breath at the sight of the handwriting.

It isn't, she thought unbelievingly. It can't be—

Her hands were trembling as she tore open the envelope and drew out the paper from inside. It was one lone sheet, with the hasty, boyish scrawl slanted across the page in the old familiar way, and as she read it, it was like hearing a beloved voice she had thought she would never hear again:

Dear Lynn—

Ernie got a letter from Nancy the other day, telling him about the tough time the kids have been giving you, and he was so broiling mad he passed it on to me, and I'm broiling mad, too. I can't imagine how anybody would think you could be mixed up in a robbery! It's the craziest thing I ever heard of. If there's anything I can do to help you straighten things out, let me know. Spring vacation starts next month, and I'll be seeing you then.

Paul

14

"Spring vacation starts next month, and I'll be seeing you then."

The words were like a song ringing through Lynn's mind in the weeks that followed. Only one month—three weeks— two weeks—and it will be spring vacation, and Paul will be home. He'll be home, and he's written me, and he'll be coming to see me, and everything will be all right! Paul's written me, and in only a couple of weeks he'll be home!

She kept the song in her mind at school, when she walked alone across the yard or ate a solitary lunch in the cafeteria, or when she heard the other girls deep in discussion of the Presentation Ball. "Paul will be home!" It rang within her, a hopeful little voice lifting her out of her unhappiness and helping her over her loneliness and making time pass more quickly. "He's written me, and he's not angry any longer, and everything will be the way it used to be!"

And yet at night, when she lay in bed, she was not so sure. She knew Paul so well, the way he was when someone was hurt and needed help. There were so many incidents to remember—the time he had helped Ernie make the football team, the way he had first taken Brenda to the dance when she had no other escort—Paul Kingsley, defender of the weak, champion of the underdog. It did not mean he felt any great affection for them personally.

Lynn felt her face grow hot as she remembered how angry she had been with him for taking Brenda to that first dance. Paul had tried to explain at the time and make her understand that it was not a personal thing. Now she realized, with an ache in her heart, that he had been telling the truth, and that very fact made the joy she felt in his letter fade a little in its light. If he could help other people without really caring about them, he could offer to help her in the same way.

And spring vacation was the time of the Presentation Ball. It was the final week of the debutante year, and everyone was talking about it, even people who had no connection with the debutantes. The whole town would be invited. The party was to be held at the Country Club. Lynn had overheard the plans so many times during the past weeks that she knew each detail by heart—the name of the orchestra that would be hired for the evening, and the way the ballroom would be decorated with gold streamers and fresh spring flowers, and the amount of punch that was to be ordered, and the kind of dresses the girls would wear—all different styles, and yet all ankle length and unrelieved white. The girls would be presented one at a time. They would walk slowly down the stairs at the far end of the ballroom, and their fathers would meet them at the foot of the steps with armloads of red roses, and then, after they had been formally introduced to society, their escorts would come forward and claim them for the first grand waltz.

And Brenda's escort, Lynn thought miserably, will be

Paul. She knew it as surely as she had ever known anything.

But still he said he would see me. He really said it—"I'll be seeing you"—and Paul always meant what he said. Lynn concentrated on that thought, holding it tightly to her when her loneliness was the worst.

When Ernie arrived home, the last week in March, his first greeting was to tell her, "Paul says he'll be over as soon as he gets his gear unpacked." And still she was not prepared when the doorbell rang, and she went to answer it and Paul was there.

"Hi!"

He was the same as ever, stocky and blue-eyed, and one eyebrow still went up a little when he spoke. The sight of him was so sudden and yet so completely familiar that Lynn stood staring at him, unable to say a word.

"Hi!" Paul said again, rather shyly. He started to step forward and then he hesitated. "Are you going to slam the door in my face?"

It was the same question he had asked after their quarrel, so long ago it seemed. Lynn smiled and found herself giving the same answer she had then.

"No, of course not. I never slam doors in people's faces. Come in, Paul."

They stood awkwardly in the hall a moment, and then Lynn said, "Come on into the living room and sit down." She found her heart was beating wildly. Trying to cover her confusion, she said the first thing that came into her head. "You look fine. You must be having a good time at college. I even think you've grown taller."

"Well, you look like you've lost weight." Paul was giving

195

her critical inspection. "You're too thin. Have you been sick?"

"Not recently." Lynn answered, seating herself on the sofa and motioning him down beside her. "I had a round of flu at Christmas time, and I guess I haven't snapped all the way back yet. And—and, as Nancy wrote Ernie—things haven't been too easy at school."

Paul nodded. "So I understand. What is this crazy thing about anyway, Lynn? What started all this mess?"

"Well, you've heard about the robbery." Lynn said uneasily. "I was right there when it happened, and then, afterward, when I stood up for Dirk, everybody sort of thought—that is, they assumed—I'd been mixed up in it somehow. There wasn't any proof of it, of course, so I wasn't actually accused; it just made everybody uncomfortable with me. I don't know exactly how to describe it—it—it just—"

"Why, that's ridiculous!" Paul's blue eyes were dark with anger. "Who in the world would ever start a rumor like that?"

"I—" Lynn faltered. "I don't know."

"You do too know, Lynn Chambers, and if you're not going to tell him, I am!" Dodie stood in the doorway, her own eyes blazing. "It was Brenda Peterson, that's who! She's been insisting that Lynn told Dirk about the money being in the car, and she's been talking everyone else into believing it too."

"Brenda? But Brenda wouldn't tell a deliberate lie to get somebody else in trouble," Paul said. "I'd swear she wouldn't; she's not that kind of a girl. If Brenda spread a story like that she must really have believed it herself." He raised his eyes to meet Lynn's. "What is your connection with this Masters fellow, anyway? Are you—are you in love with him?"

"No!" Lynn said passionately. "I'm *not!* Why does everyone keep insisting I am?"

"Then what were you doing, chasing him across the parking lot in the first place?" Paul asked. "How did you happen to be there at all?"

"I had a necklace," Lynn said. "I was trying to return it to him. I never got a chance to."

"A necklace? You mean one he gave you?"

"Yes," Lynn answered. "It was his mother's. It—" She hesitated, hating to continue.

"You might as well tell him the whole story," Dodie broke in briskly. "How Dirk gave it to you and when and all the rest of it. If Paul's going to know any of it, he should know it all."

Lynn felt her face growing red. "All right," she said miserably. "I guess I don't have much choice."

It was the second time she had repeated the story. The time before, when she had told Dodie, she had given all the details—the way she had felt that evening after the fight with Paul; how she had seen him in the treasure hunt crowd outside the party; the way she had cried, and the things she had said, and the things Dirk had said in return. She tried to skip over these things now, but Dodie would not let her. She still stood in the doorway, following her sister's every word, and if Lynn tried to omit any portion of the story, Dodie would interrupt with, "Now, Lynn, that's not the way you told it to me. Go ahead and tell the whole thing."

By the time she had finished, Lynn's face was burning and she was ready to burst into tears.

There was a moment of silence in the room. Then Paul reached over and touched her hand. "Did—did you really feel that way? I mean, about me?"

Lynn nodded wordlessly.

"Then why didn't you tell me? All you had to do was call me. I felt so rotten about that fight we had. All you had to do was give me the nod, and I would have been here so fast it wouldn't have been funny."

"You would?" Lynn stared at him. "Then why didn't *you* call *me*?"

"I guess for the same reason you didn't call. I was stubborn. I didn't want to be the one to apologize." He hesitated, and when he spoke again, his voice trembled uncertainly. "I—I'll apologize now, Lynn."

"I don't want you to apologize," Lynn said. "There's nothing to apologize for. We were both jealous, and we were both wrong, but I was the wronger. I went ahead and accepted the necklace from Dirk. I knew I shouldn't at the time, but I did, so really I guess I've brought this whole mess on myself."

"Well," Paul asked, "what are we going to do about it?"

'To do about it?" Lynn stared at him as though she were not sure she had heard him correctly. "You mean you think there's something we can do?"

"All along, you've been saying this guy is innocent," Paul said sensibly. "That's one of the things that's got you messed up in this, in the first place. Surely you've got some reason for thinking so."

"I don't just think so," Lynn said, "I *know* so. And what's more, I know who *did* take the wallet and how he did it." Leaning forward, she began eagerly to tell the story of Brad and Dirk and the gym bag.

When she had finished, she leaned back expectantly, waiting for Paul's reaction.

"But that's all a lot of speculation," he said. "You've figured out how this Brad might have taken it, but you don't have any proof. You don't really have anything to go on except the way you feel about it."

Lynn was disappointed. "Then you don't think we can do anything, after all?"

"No," Paul said. "Not on that. Not on just what you told me." He stood up. "Where did you say Dirk Masters works?"

"At Burton's Garage." Lynn got up, too. "What are you going to do?"

"Talk to him." Paul glanced at his watch and started toward the door. "It's four-thirty now. I should be able to just nab him, if he gets off at five. That's the garage on 40th, isn't it?"

"Yes." Lynn caught up with him at the door. "Wait, Paul! I'm going with you."

"There's no reason for you to do that. I can talk to him by myself."

"No, I want to be there," Lynn said stubbornly. "Please, Paul. I'm concerned in this, too."

Paul hesitated. Then he said, "O.K., if you insist, but I still think it might be better if I went alone. Sometimes fellows can straighten things out better, man-to-man, than they can with a girl around. Especially a girl they've both been going with."

"I want to be there when you first meet him," Lynn insisted. "I don't want any fighting or anything. Dirk has a terrible temper sometimes."

Paul gave her a half smile. "Come on then, Little Peace-maker. But there's not going to be any fighting. I should think Dirk would be pretty glad at this point to have some-body trying to help him."

"But why *are* you?" Lynn asked in bewilderment. "You've never liked Dirk at all. You called him a 'tough little smart aleck' when we talked about him at Christmas time."

Paul nodded in agreement "And I haven't changed my opinion. But even a 'tough little smart aleck' can get a raw deal. You know him better than I do, and you say he's inno-cent. You wouldn't be saying that unless you really thought so. And if you think so, that's good enough for me."

They reached the garage a little before five and parked beside Dirk's car. They were there waiting for him when he came out after work.

Dirk regarded them with surprise. He nodded at Lynn, and then turned his full gaze upon Paul. "What's this, a reception committee? What are you doing here, Kingsley? I thought you were at college."

"I am," Paul said. "It's spring vacation. I came home to find Lynn as thin as a toothpick and on the verge of a ner-vous breakdown, and I'm going to try to help her get things straightened out."

There was a hint of the old sarcasm in Dirk's voice as he answered. "What do you think you're going to do—snap your fingers and make everything all right?"

"Of course not, but maybe we can figure out some-thing."

Paul put a companionable hand on Dirk's shoulder. "Let's sit down. Want to make it in my car or yours?"

Dirk was silent a moment. Then he stepped forward and opened the door of his car. "O.K.," he said, "climb in. It may not be much, Kingsley, but it's home."

It was a feeble joke, but it served its purpose. Suddenly, the tension was eased among them. They climbed into the car, Lynn in back and the boys in front.

"Well, here's the story," Dirk said. "See what you can make of it."

It was in substance the same story Lynn had told Paul, with a little more added. Dirk described Brad and told something about his background.

"He's a couple of years older than I am and has an apartment of his own. He never talks about his folks—I don't even know if he has any. He doesn't have a job, but he seems to get along all right. He always has plenty of money for a good time." Dirk shook his head. "I don't know why I let myself get mixed up with the guy in the first place, except that he had a car, and I didn't, and he was always wanting me to help him with it. And he acted like he liked me and really wanted me along. You wouldn't understand that, Kingsley, always being the head of everything at school—but when you're not part of things, it can make you feel kind of good, having somebody act like he wants you."

Paul asked, "Does he have a police record? Do you know if he's ever been involved in something like this before?"

"I don't know," Dirk answered slowly. "Now that I think about it, he might have been. He was always talking about 'big deals,' laughing at kids like Ronnie Tinner with his drugstore job after school and hinting about how there were easier ways to make money, if you were smart enough to find them. I never listened to him much. I always figured he was just talking big to impress me."

They sat in silence a moment. Then Paul asked, "Why don't we go over there now?"

"Where?"

"To Brad's apartment. Let's just walk in and confront him with this thing and see what he has to say."

"Are you crazy?" Dirk was staring at him. "He'll laugh in our faces!"

"Maybe so," Paul said. "Maybe not. We can't tell till we get there. There are two of us now, you know. Sometimes it's easier to laugh at one person than at two."

Dirk said, "It won't do any good. He probably won't even let us in the door."

"Then we'll walk in." Paul grinned. "I was captain of the high-school football team, Masters. I think I can push open a door, if I have to. And from what Lynn tells me, you have a pretty good temper yourself. I think with both of us, one on either side of him, Brad Morgan might not think the situation was quite so funny."

After a moment, Dirk grinned, too. "Maybe he wouldn't, at that. At least it would be worth a try." He turned to Paul, and slowly his grin faded. "You're sure you want to, Kingsley? I mean, there's no reason why *you* should have to—"

"Of course, I want to," Paul answered easily. "I wouldn't miss it for the world. After all, it's my idea."

He reached into his pocket, pulled out a set of keys and tossed them to Lynn.

"Drive my car home, will you, Lynn? I'll ride over to Brad's apartment with Dirk."

"But I'm coming, too!" Lynn exclaimed. "I want to be in on this."

The boys turned toward her with one accord, and there was the same look on both their faces.

Paul said, "I told you before, Lynn, that there are times when it's better for a girl not to be along. This is one of those times."

"But—but you might *need* me for—for something!" Lynn turned beseechingly to Dirk. "You want me to come, don't you, Dirk? After all—"

But Dirk was already sliding out of the driver's seat and opening the back door for her.

"Thanks, Princess," he said, "but Kingsley's right. You'd better go on home."

"But—but—" Lynn looked from one boy to the other and realized it was hopeless.

She sighed, took up the keys and got out of Dirk's car.

15

Lynn fidgeted through dinner that evening, with one ear open for the telephone and the other for the doorbell.

"What's the matter, Daughter? You're not eating. Aren't you feeling well?"

Lynn smiled at her father's familiar question. It was one thing that came with having a doctor in the family, every time you didn't gulp down a meal as though you were half starved, you got your temperature taken.

"No," she said, "I'm just not awfully hungry."

"Lynn was out for a drive this afternoon," her mother said pointedly. "Paul came by for her."

"Paul Kingsley?" Dr. Chambers looked pleased. "Well, is that romance going strong again? Fine, fine! But don't let excitement take away your appetite, Daughter. Growing girls need energy, you know."

Dodie, who had been unusually quiet during the meal, entered the conversation. "Did he say anything about the Presentation Ball? It's tomorrow night, you know."

"We never got around to the subject," Lynn told her.

Dodie nodded, understanding. "Well, there's still time for him to ask you."

"Yes."

Lynn thought, the Presentation Ball. She wanted to go; oh, how she wanted to go! It was the one debutante dance that was open to the public, the final big party of the debutante season, and it was supposed to be the grandest party the town had ever known. The debutantes had been practicing every afternoon all week for their grand entrance down the stairs into the ballroom, and Nancy had told her there had even been a special dancing instructor to teach them how to make their curtsies.

"I'm so sore I can hardly move," Nancy had said, laughing. "It's like doing calisthenics. You go down—down—down—until your head almost touches the ground, and then you have to come up gracefully, without falling. It's quite a trick."

"It sounds effective," Lynn had agreed. "I hope I'll be there to see it. I just might, you know. I mean, if Paul comes home and everything is like it used to be."

Nancy seemed less hopeful. "Don't count on it too much. His letter—his saying he wants to help you if he can—that's swell, of course. But he doesn't say anything about the Ball, and I happen to know Brenda is counting on going with him. She's signed him up on the list as her escort and it seems pretty well settled."

"Well," Lynn had said, "we'll see."

And thinking about it now, she still was not sure how things stood between them. Paul had been wonderful and had seemed genuinely glad to see her. He had apologized for his part in the quarrel and wanted to be friends again. But perhaps that was all he wanted now—to be friends.

Dinner had been over almost an hour when the doorbell finally rang. Lynn, who had been trying to concentrate on the evening paper, was on her feet in an instant and flew to the door to meet Paul.

When she saw him, she gave a gasp of horror. "What's happened to your hand?"

Paul's hand was wrapped to the wrist with white adhesive tape.

"Just smashed it up a little." Paul grinned at her. He looked very pleased with himself. "What an evening! Gosh! Where can we sit and talk?"

Lynn led the way into the living room and sank onto the sofa, drawing Paul down beside her. "The family's all upstairs, so you can tell me the whole story. I want to hear everything. Start at the beginning."

"Well," Paul said, "to start with, of course, we drove over to Brad Morgan's apartment."

"What was it like?" Lynn asked. "Was it a shabby place?"

"No, that surprised me. It was a ground floor apartment, in a nice neighborhood. It didn't look like the sort of place a guy would live in if he didn't have a job. We parked the car and went up and knocked on the door, but there wasn't any answer. Then we tried the door, and it was locked, so we were pretty sure Brad wasn't there."

"So you waited?" Lynn asked eagerly.

"Yes. But after a few minutes we realized that, if we just stood there in plain sight, Brad Morgan would never come home, so Dirk suggested that we climb in a window and wait inside and really take him by surprise."

Lynn's face paled. "But, Paul, that's breaking and entering! You could be arrested for something like that!"

Paul looked sheepish. "You're right, it wasn't a smart thing to do. I guess I was getting kind of carried away by the cops and robbers game. Anyway, I tagged along after Dirk, while he tried the windows, and when he found one that was open, I scrambled in after him and we stationed ourselves on either side of the front door."

"Weren't you scared to death?" Lynn asked in awe.

"I was nervous," Paul admitted, "but I wasn't exactly what you'd call scared. Not until Dirk remembered the gun."

"The gun!" Lynn cried in horror. "What gun?"

"We were standing there, waiting for Brad to arrive, when Dirk said, 'My gosh, I forgot about the pistol!' It seemed Brad Morgan had a pistol, a thirty-eight revolver. Dirk said he'd seen it lots of times. Brad was proud of it and was always showing it off, and sometimes he carried it around with him. Dirk said he'd never seen Brad use it, and he always thought he just kept it to show off with, but still, it wasn't too pleasant a thought. Brad walking in with a gun was a little different from Brad just walking in."

"It certainly was!" Lynn said shakily. "I hope you got out that window again in a hurry!"

"We started to," Brad said, "and then suddenly Dirk said, 'He usually keeps the gun in his bureau. Let's take a look and see if it's there.' I didn't want any part of that. By this time, I was plenty sorry I'd never been dope enough to come inside in the first place. I said, 'Let's not go poking around. Let's just get out and wait in the car.' I was already swinging my legs out the window when Dirk let out a shout, "Come here, Kingsley! Look what Brad has in his drawer! It's a whole jewelry store!'"

"What did he mean?" Lynn asked in bewilderment

"Just that. Honestly, Lynn, I never saw anything like it in my whole life! Dirk had pulled open the top drawer of the bureau, looking for the gun, and, instead, he'd found enough jewelry to stock a store—watches, pins, necklaces—piles and piles of them! It was like opening a pirates' treasure chest. And back behind them was a pile of empty wallets."

"What did you do then?" Lynn breathed.

"Well, the first thing I did was to pull my legs back in the window and go over to that bureau to get a look for myself. The next thing I did was to say, 'Let's call the police.' Dirk said, 'We can't call from here—Brad doesn't have a telephone.' And then we heard the key turning in the door."

"Oh, no!" Lynn felt her heart lurch. "Was it Brad?"

Paul nodded. "There wasn't time to move. We just stood there while the door swung open and Brad came in. He saw Dirk first and said, 'What the devil are you doing here, Masters?' And then he saw the drawer open. And then he saw me."

"The gun—" Lynn began.

"We didn't take time to think about the gun; we just dove at him, Dirk and I, one from each side. And boy, Lynn, that guy was built like a bull! I've played football, but I've never tried to tackle anybody like that. He just wouldn't go down. He threw himself sideways and slammed Dirk against the wall, then started across the room toward the bureau, dragging me right along with him. And then, of course, we knew where the gun was."

"In the bureau?"

"Yes, otherwise he wouldn't be headed there in such a hurry. Dirk yelled, 'You hang onto him, Kingsley, while I get it!' Well, I knew I couldn't possibly hang onto Brad—it would have been like hanging onto a charging rhino. So I hauled back my fist to sock him, and just then he whirled out of the way and my fist smacked right into the wall.

"That pretty well wrecked one hand, and before I could think to use the other one, Brad gave me one hard sock in the midsection and down I went, flat on the floor. That would have been that if it hadn't been for Dirk. Brad was hauling back his foot, aiming a kick at my head, when Dirk said, 'O.K., Brad, if you move again, you're going to be sorry.' And there he was, holding the pistol."

"Thank goodness!" Lynn breathed. She felt weak with relief. "Oh, Paul, thank goodness!"

"Thank goodness is right." Paul said with a grin. "The gun had been far back in the drawer, behind the wallets. When Brad saw it in Dirk's hand, he stopped where he was. He said, 'You wouldn't use that, Masters.' And Dirk, (he was shaking like a leaf, with that pistol wobbling back and forth; I don't think he could have pulled the trigger if his life depended on it) said, 'Wouldn't I? After the way you left me to take the blame for taking the Peterson girl's wallet?' Brad said, 'I didn't like doing that, but it was the only thing I could do. You didn't have a record—I knew you'd get off light—but I would have gone to jail.' So Dirk said, 'You heard him, Kingsley. You can tell the police what he said.' And I dragged myself up off the floor and said, 'Sure I can.' So Dirk kept Brad covered while I went next door and phoned the police."

"Oh, Paul!" Lynn said weakly. "I feel as though I'd been through it all myself. So the police came and arrested Brad?"

"That's right," Paul said. "That stuff in the drawer was enough to convict him on half a dozen different counts. There's been a whole siege of housebreakings lately, and they're sure that's where most of that jewelry came from. They have to check it out, of course, but as far as we're concerned, everything's settled. Dirk's cleared of the schoolyard robbery, and, of course, you're cleared of any connection with it. And it all took less than an hour."

"An hour!" Lynn exclaimed. "You mean all this happened this afternoon, and you let me worry myself sick all through dinner without even phoning to tell me about it?"

"I'm sorry," Paul said. "I probably should have called, but there was so much to do. I had to get this hand bandaged up, and then I went over to the Petersons' and asked Brenda if she was responsible for the way the kids have been treating you."

"You didn't expect her to say yes, did you?" Lynn asked.

"She did say yes."

Lynn stared at him in amazement. "You mean, she actually admitted it?"

"Sure she did. She looked pretty horrified, too, when she heard the real story. She said she'd get on the phone tonight and call every single one of the debutantes and tell them neither you nor Dirk had anything to do with the robbery. That's nineteen girls she has to call, and each of them will go to school on Monday and tell nineteen others, and if I know the way girls talk, by the end of the day, your reputation is going to be as clean as a whistle."

"Oh, Paul, thank you!" It was as though the weight of pain and loneliness which had hung over her for three long months was suddenly lifted, and the abruptness of the release left her lightheaded. Lynn felt tears of relief and gratitude filling her eyes. "Oh, Paul—"

"Hey," he said, "don't start crying. Everything's O.K. now. You don't have to cry."

He pulled her toward him, and she moved forward, and then his arms were around her and everything was all right—really all right. Lynn took a deep breath and relaxed completely for the first time in months. She thought this is where I belong. I never want to move again. And yet even as she thought it she was drawing back a little, so she could see his face. And what she saw there was what she wanted to see.

"I missed you," he said huskily.

"And I missed you," Lynn whispered. "I never missed anybody so much in my whole life."

Paul still had his arm around her a few minutes later when Ernie came thudding in.

"Don't mind me, lovebirds. I just live here."

"Look who's talking!" Paul said with a grin. "I bet you were pretty darned glad to see your own girl, weren't you?"

"You're not kidding." Ernie grinned back. "In fact, I'm heading for her place right now, to help cart a load of glasses over to the Country Club. The Presentation Ball's tomorrow." He paused at the door and then added in a very offhand manner, "Why don't the four of us double? The whole town's invited, you know."

Lynn was afraid to meet her brother's eyes, for fear the gratitude would be too obvious on her face. She waited tensely for Paul's answer.

It was a moment in coming. When he did speak, it was slowly.

"I—I can't, Ern. I've already promised to take Brenda Peterson."

"Hey, what's the big idea?" Ernie said in surprise. "Lynn sat home all Christmas while you beaued around the Peterson girl. This is the big dance of the year, of any year, for that matter. How can you refuse to take her?"

"Well, when you put it that way—" Paul turned to Lynn. "I want to take you, you know that. The thing is, I started taking Brenda to the Christmas parties and kind of got stuck in the role of escort. When she asked me if I'd take her to the Presentation Ball, I couldn't get out of it very well. Besides, at the time you and I—"

"I know," Lynn said hastily.

"So I said I would, and she could never in the world get another escort this late. She's got her dress and shoes and everything, and they have been rehearsing the presentations for weeks. If Brenda doesn't make her debut now, because she doesn't have an escort, she'll be the laughing stock of the school."

"And what about Lynn?" Ernie demanded, angry now.

"Don't you owe her anything? It's just great to be the Good Samaritan, but you can carry the thing too far. You're a good guy, Paul, and I know you've helped *me* out plenty of times, but Lynn's my sister, and I think she's getting the rough side of this deal."

Paul said, "I don't know. I—I just don't know. I want to do the right thing."

He looked so miserable and confused that Lynn felt a quick surge of sympathy. After all, this was Paul, Paul as she knew him best, warmhearted and eager to help everyone who seemed in need of him. It was the way he was and the way he would always be, and if she wanted Paul, she must take that too, because it was part of him. Perhaps even the part that had made her fall in love with him in the first place.

So now she smiled and gave his good hand a quick pat.

"That's all right," she said, as easily as she could. "Of course, you can't back out now. I understand."

Ernie shot her a glance of complete amazement. "But I know you want to go to the Ball! You're dying to—"

"Please, Ern," Lynn said softly. "I appreciate what you're trying to do, but this is something between Paul and me—for us to decide."

Ernie shook his head in bewilderment. "I'll never understand women."

He turned toward the door, and Paul rose to follow him. He gave Lynn a last, almost pleading look.

"You do understand? I mean, you know it's not that I don't want to take you."

Lynn said, "Don't worry. I understand. I really do."

And she did. That was the hard part of it. She could not be angry or resentful with Paul because she did understand. He had made a promise, and a promise meant a lot to Paul— more, perhaps, than it did to other people.

And yet the anger and resentment were there, deep inside her. They needed only a breath to stir them into flame, and that breath came an hour later, when the doorbell rang again.

Lynn had been playing checkers with Dodie. The sound of the bell startled her, and then she sprang to her feet with a thrill of joy. It's Paul, she thought. He's come back! He's thought it over and changed his mind. That's the only reason he would come back this evening!

Which was why it was so much more of a shock to

open the door and see Brenda Peterson.

The two girls stood looking at each other a moment. Then Brenda said, "May I come in?"

"Why, yes," Lynn replied automatically. "Please do. I—I was just surprised to see you."

"I suppose you are." Brenda stepped into the hall and shut the door behind her. "I won't sit down. I can't stay long enough for that. Mother's outside, waiting for me in the car. I've come to apologize to you for the things I said about you at school."

Lynn opened her mouth to answer and then closed it again. There was nothing she could think of to say.

"I really did think you must have some connection with the theft," Brenda continued awkwardly. "I didn't mean to spread a story that was untrue. But now that I think back on it, to be perfectly honest, I guess I did kind of jump on the situation and—and sort of push it. You were always so popular, Lynn, and I never was. You—well, I've heard people speak of you as Princess of the Hill. Maybe I was jealous. *I* was never accepted in anything unless my mother engineered it."

Lynn was flustered. She did not know what to say. The entire year long she had disliked this girl with all the passion that was in her. Because of Brenda, she had suffered through the unhappiest few months of her life. She had even lain awake nights, thinking of unpleasant things to say to her if the opportunity ever arose. But now, suddenly confronted with her, Lynn could think of nothing to say at all.

Dodie, however, was never one to be speechless. She had followed Lynn into the hall and now stepped to her sister's side.

"You never had to be like that," she said sharply. "You *let* your mother engineer things. You just drifted along and let her run things for you and never even tried to be a person yourself. No wonder people didn't like you; there just didn't seem to be anything there to like."

"Dodie!" Lynn was horrified. "How can you say something like that—to *anybody!*"

Brenda's pale little face grew a shade paler. But she accepted the statement without cringing. "I realize that now. This year, for the first time, I've had friends, people who liked me and wanted me with them." The words rang familiarly in Lynn's ears. She wondered where she had heard them before and then, suddenly, she heard Dirk's voice saying the same thing. He had said, "If you're not part of things, it can make you feel awfully good having somebody act like he wants you."

They were lonely, she thought. Lonely. Both of them—such different people—in such different circumstances—and both of them were lonely.

She opened her mouth to speak, but Brenda was still talking. "It was as if, for the first time, I really belonged. You can't imagine how I felt when Mother first told me that Paul Kingsley, the most popular boy in town almost, had called to ask to take me to the debutante parties."

"Paul called *you?*" Before Lynn could stop her, Dodie had burst again into the conversation. "Oh, honestly, Brenda, you can't make us believe that. We know for a fact that your mother was the one who called Paul."

"What?"

"Dodie—" Lynn cried helplessly, "don't—"

But Dodie was not to be halted. "It was a pretty sneaky

trick too! You knew he was the kind of boy who would help anybody in trouble, so you got your mother to phone him and say that you couldn't get anybody else to take you to the dance. And all the while Paul was supposed to be going steady with my sister."

Brenda's face was dead white. "That's not true! I never told Mother to phone Paul! I thought—she told me—" Her chin trembled. "Then that's why—I wondered—I couldn't imagine why he would date me when nobody else ever had. I—I actually believed—it was because he liked me."

"He does like you!" Lynn cried, frightened at the sight of the girl's stricken face. "Don't listen to Dodie, Brenda—she doesn't know what she's talking about. Paul does like you. He's told me so himself."

But Brenda was not listening to her. She had turned toward the door and was fumbling with the knob. "I'm sorry," she said again in a muffled little voice. "I guess I owe you two apologies, one because of the business of the wallet and one for Mother's calling Paul. I hope you believe me, Lynn. I didn't know about that. I thought—all along I thought—*he* asked *me!*"

And then she was gone, running down the steps and across the lawn to the waiting car. She might have been crying, it was hard to tell. If she was, it was silent crying, because Lynn could hear her voice, small and steady across the night, as she joined her mother in the car.

Mrs. Peterson asked, "Did you and Lynn straighten everything out between you?"

And Brenda said, "Yes, everything's straight now," and got in and shut the door.

"Well," Dodie shifted uneasily from one foot to another, "I guess maybe I overdid it a little."

"I guess maybe you did." Lynn regarded her sister coldly. "How could you, Dodie? How could you have said such cruel, horrible things?"

"They were true," Dodie defended herself. "You know they were. Mrs. Peterson did arrange for Paul to date Brenda. Your whole year has been ruined because of that Peterson girl. Why should you be so concerned about her precious feelings?"

"I don't know," Lynn answered slowly, surprised herself. "Maybe because *I* was cruel to her too, you know. I didn't think of it as cruelty at the time, but it was. For years I snubbed her and left her out of things and joked about her with the others behind her back, and I never thought how she might be feeling about it. I never stopped to think how lonely she might be."

"I'm sorry," Dodie said in a small voice. "I guess I let my tongue get away from me. It seems to be a fault of mine."

She sounded so ashamed of herself that Lynn did not have the heart to scold her any further. "What's done is done," she said as lightly as she could. "I know you were angry on my account and just didn't think. I don't suppose too much harm was done. And—thank you for being so loyal, Dodie."

But when Lynn went back into the living room and tumbled down onto the sofa, Brenda's face swam in front of her, small and colorless and big-eyed. She picked up a book and stared at the pages without really seeing them. She heard the soft little voice again—"I thought all along that *he* was asking *me!*"

Perhaps she did, Lynn thought. Maybe her mother didn't tell her. It is just the sort of thing Mrs. Peterson might do—arrange for an escort for her daughter and then not mention the fact. Mrs. Peterson was so used to running things that she ran Brenda automatically, without even thinking about it, always so certain that she was doing what was best.

And was it best? Perhaps, in a way it was. Lynn thought back upon the girl Brenda had become in the past year. What was it Ernie had said about her? "Since the debutante parties started, she's been like another girl, kind of sparkly and bright-looking, almost pretty." And that from Ernie, who never had eyes for any girl except Nancy.

Going with Paul could do that for a girl, Lynn knew, because she had often felt it herself. Being liked and accepted by a crowd, having a handsome, popular boy dating you—it could make you believe in yourself when nothing else could.

It's turned Brenda into a real person, Lynn thought now. All the kids seem to like her. Maybe if I hadn't been so busy hating her, I might have liked her myself.

She tried to focus her attention on the book, but her mind kept slipping away from it and turning back to Brenda.

I do wish Dodie hadn't said what she did tonight, Lynn thought regretfully. After all, Brenda came here to apologize. That must have been hard enough for her to do, without having all that other business thrown in her face. I hope it didn't hurt her too much.

She thought, I wish we could go back half an hour and start over again. . . . But, of course, that was impossible.

16

When she woke up the next morning, Lynn had the uncomfortable feeling that something was wrong. For a moment, she could not remember what it was. Then, suddenly, it came back to her—the scene with Brenda the night before—and now, in the bright morning light, it seemed doubly unnecessary and unpleasant.

I could call her, Lynn thought, and apologize.

But she knew there would not be much point in that. The damage had been done. Calling to hash things over would do nothing but make matters worse.

Pushing the incident from her mind, Lynn dressed and went down to breakfast.

Everyone else was already at the table when she came in.

"—so that will be that," Dodie was saying.

"What will be what?" Lynn asked, sitting down and picking up her glass of orange juice.

"Dodie says," her father answered with an undisguised note of satisfaction in his voice, "that she and her friends aren't planning to be debutantes next year."

"They're not!" Lynn exclaimed. "But, Dodie, I thought you said you'd die if you couldn't be a debutante."

"Maybe I did," Dodie admitted placidly. "But a person can change her mind, can't she? And a lot of things have happened this year."

"Like Ronnie Turner?" Ernie's eyes twinkled mischievously. "Looks like our baby sister is growing up, Lynn."

"Looks like," Lynn agreed. But the surprise remained. "Is that the reason, Dodie? Because you don't think Ronnie would be included at the parties?"

"Oh, that's part of it," Dodie admitted, "but it's not just Ronnie alone. It's that a lot of nice kids would be left out because their families didn't have the right backgrounds. Until I met Ronnie and his friends, I didn't know those kids counted. But they do. Some of them are nicer than the kids from the Hill."

Lynn nodded, thinking of Anne and her friends.

"But what about the rest of your crowd? Do they feel the same way?"

"We've been talking about it," Dodie answered. "Some of them agree with me and are going to stay out, just for the principle of the thing. Some of the others who have fathers in the Rotary with Daddy," she gave her father a sideways glance, "have run into disapproval at home. I can't imagine why!"

"Well, I can!" Dr. Chambers said with a roar of delighted laughter. "I've been hounding those poor fellows all year about how undemocratic this debutante business is. I guess maybe I've got some results."

"Anyway," Dodie continued, between mouthfuls of toast, "there are so many of the Hill crowd who don't want to be debs for one reason or another that there aren't enough left to have a decent party. So I guess that will be that."

Mrs. Chambers shook her head. "Poor Mrs. Peterson, having her pet project fold in its second year. She'll be heartbroken."

"I doubt it," Lynn said. "After all, her whole point was to bring Brenda into society, and she's done that, so she's accomplished her purpose."

At the mention of Brenda, guilt flared up within her again. But the harm has been done, she told herself determinedly. There's no sense in worrying about it now.

The day dragged by slowly. Paul phoned during the morning. He suggested they go out to dinner the following evening and then to a movie and maybe dancing afterward. Lynn knew he was trying to make up to her for taking Brenda to the Ball.

She agreed to his plans, trying to sound enthusiastic and somehow failing.

"Hey," Paul said in a worried voice, "you're not mad, are you? I mean, you said it was all right for me to take Brenda tonight."

"I know I did," Lynn told him. "No, of course I'm not mad. Have a good time, and I'll see you tomorrow."

"You know, you don't have to sit home," Paul continued. "You don't need an escort for the Ball, if you're not a debutante. You could go with your folks. That way, you'd get to see the girls make their debuts and be in on all the excitement."

Lynn sighed. "You know the way Daddy feels about the debutantes. He'd never go to the Ball, even if I begged him to. The plans for tomorrow night sound grand, though. We'll have a lot of fun."

"Sure we will," Paul said heartily. "Well, I'll see you then."

"See you then," Lynn echoed. But tomorrow seemed forever away as she replaced the phone and wandered aimlessly back, to her room.

She considered going over to Nancy's, but she knew her friend would be busy getting ready for her debut. Even Ernie had been forbidden at Nancy's this morning and had gone out to play tennis with some other boys. Lynn sighed and decided to straighten her dresser drawers, a chore she had been putting off for weeks. At least it would fill the time.

She finished the drawers by noon and started on her closet. When that was finished, she sat down and wrote two letters she had owed for ages and sewed some buttons on a blouse and manicured her nails.

In the middle of the afternoon, Dirk stopped by. He did not even come in, just stood on the porch and talked a moment, but there was an ease about him she had not seen before. For once, he did not seem to be fighting her or himself or anyone. All the complex emotions that had formerly boiled within him—resentment and pride and anger—seemed to have given way to a kind of quiet.

He did not say much. He just held out his hand and said, "Thanks for everything."

"You're welcome," Lynn replied softly. She took the hand he offered her and returned the pressure of his fingers.

"Paul told you how it all worked out, didn't he?"

"He stopped by last night," Lynn said. "He told me all about the fight and the jewelry you found. And he said Brad admitted taking Brenda's wallet."

"He admitted taking the jewelry, too," Dirk said. "I've been down at the police station all morning. They wanted to know all about Brad. There wasn't much I could tell them, though, except that he was a guy who wasn't as lucky as I was. He didn't have a family and friends to straighten him out when he got headed in the wrong direction." He did not release her hand. He stood holding it a moment, as though trying to think how to put something into words. Finally he said, "Paul Kingsley's a pretty swell fellow. I see why you fell for him. I didn't know him before, but I see it now—why it would be a guy like that over me."

"I wish you wouldn't—" Lynn started to withdraw her hand, but Dirk tightened his grip.

"No, wait. Let me finish. I just want you to know I'm not giving up. I'm going to work like the dickens to be the kind of a guy a girl like you would care for. I mean, heck, I've got expensive tastes. I can't settle for an ordinary girl; I want a princess! I guess I'd better buckle down and earn one."

He was making a joke of it, and Lynn found herself smiling back at him and liking him better than she ever had before. "Wait a minute," she urged.

Breaking away from him, she ran into the house and upstairs to her bedroom, returning a moment later with the small cardboard box.

"It's your mother's necklace. I should have given it back to you before, but with all the confusion of the robbery, I just never seemed to get a chance to," she said, handing it to him. "You'll want it, Dirk. Some day there will be somebody else you'll want to give it to."

Dirk stood looking at the box a moment and then thrust it into his pocket. "Maybe so," he said gruffly. "Right now, it doesn't seem possible, but some day maybe there will be."

The rest of the day passed more quickly, for Ernie came

home from his tennis and sat around talking for a while before he went up to get dressed for the evening, and then Dodie wandered in, and soon afterward Mrs. Chambers was lighting the dining room candles and Rosalie was announcing dinner.

And then, all too soon, dinner was over and the family was breaking up. Dr. Chambers had an evening call to make, and Ernie left in a flash of black tuxedo, to pick up Nancy for the Ball, and after a while Ronnie stopped by for Dodie. Lynn found herself in front of the television set again, while her mother sat in the chair at the desk, going through a pile of bills and totaling the month's household expenditures.

I don't usually mind watching television, Lynn told herself sternly. I don't know why I should feel so restless tonight.

But she did know. Tonight was the Presentation Ball. The knowledge was deep within her, and she could not break away from it or focus her attention on anything else. Tonight was the Ball, and Paul was taking Brenda. Paul would be wearing his tuxedo. She could picture him now, and she could see Brenda with him. Was she pretty? Probably, if she was with Paul. "Sparkly," Ernie had called her. Well, she was making her debut tonight, her entrance into society. She would certainly be sparkly tonight.

Lynn squirmed unhappily, trying to force her attention on the television show. What were they doing now? She glanced at her watch. Four minutes to eight. The girls were being presented at nine o'clock, so they were probably at the Country Club already. Maybe they were just getting there. Paul would be pulling his car into the parking lot. Now he would be getting out, opening the door for Brenda, helping her out. The music would be flooding the night, and crowds would be arriving, and Paul would probably be steering Brenda in the back way, so nobody would see her until she was officially presented and came gracefully down the stairs to receive her red roses.

The doorbell rang.

The sound cut through Lynn's thoughts with such suddenness that for a moment she did not know what it was. When it registered, she did not have any particular reaction. After all, there was no one who would be calling on her.

Her mother glanced up with a little frown of annoyance, saying, "Get the door, will you, dear? I'm right in the middle of adding a row of figures."

"All right." Lynn rose slowly, stretched and made her way unhurriedly to the door. When she opened it her eyes opened wide with astonishment.

"Paul! What are you doing here?"

"What does it look like?" he returned with a grin. "I've come to take you to the dance. Run upstairs and throw on a gown and slap on your eyelashes, or whatever girls do on occasions like this, and let's get going. That is, if you don't mind having a date with a bandaged hand."

Lynn stared at him in bewilderment. "What are you talking about? Where's Brenda?"

"She's sick," Paul explained. "The poor kid must have flu or something. She looked kind of pale when I got there, but I thought it was just excitement. Her mother was fussing around so much, it would be enough to make anybody nervous. But then, when we were in the car, we hardly got out of the driveway before Brenda asked me to take her back again. She said she felt terrible."

"But she couldn't be sick!" Lynn exclaimed. "Not when she's going to make her debut. Why, she'd have to be half dead to miss that, and there was nothing wrong with her when she came by yesterday evening."

"She said she was sick," Paul said. "I didn't argue with her. I guess the girl knows how she feels. Her mother had left for the dance herself, by the time we got back, so there wasn't any argument about it."

"You mean you just left her all by herself in the house?" Lynn cried in horror. "If she's that sick, you should have stayed there and called a doctor."

"She told me not to," Paul said defensively. "She said it wasn't anything serious, that she had a headache and an upset stomach and she thought she was getting the flu. She said she wanted to be left alone, to take a few aspirin and go to bed, and if I hurried, I could get over here and pick you up in time to make it to the Ball." He looked a little sheepish. "I guess maybe that sounded like too good an idea. I didn't argue about it I just said O.K., and got in the car and came over."

He looked so handsome, standing there in his tuxedo, his blue eyes hopeful, one eyebrow rising a little when he talked. And he was so pleased at the way things had worked out! Looking at him, Lynn felt the worry that had closed around her heart loosen and drop away. There was no question in her mind now about whom Paul wanted to take to the dance. The happiness on his face left no doubt of that.

"It's tough luck for Brenda," he was saying easily, "poor kid, having to miss her own debut. And it's rotten of me to feel this way, I guess, but darn it, Lynn, a guy wants to take his own girl to something like this! And now it's worked out so I can."

A guy wants to take his own girl. There it was, in words —*his own girl*.

Lynn caught at the words and hugged them to her, and it was with her own answering happiness that she found herself able to smile at him and shake her head and say, "No, Paul. It didn't work out this way. Brenda made it work out."

He looked at her without understanding. "What do you mean? I told you, she's sick."

"No, she isn't," Lynn said quietly. "She's no more sick than I am. She knows you are just taking her because her mother asked you to, and she's giving you an out. She's pretending she's sick to give you a chance to take me instead."

"But why would she do a thing like that? I've taken her to dances before because her mother asked me to."

"But Brenda didn't know it then," Lynn explained. "She knows it now because Dodie told her. I was sorry about it, but I never guessed she would do something like this. I never knew she had that much initiative!" She paused as the picture formed in her mind. "Good heavens, Paul, can't you visualize the scene when Mrs. Peterson gets home tonight, after Brenda doesn't turn up at the Ball? A whole year of preparation for Brenda's debut, and then she stays home and goes to bed instead!"

"I didn't think Brenda ever stood up to her mother," Paul said. "Especially not about something important."

"I didn't either," Lynn said slowly. "You know, I think maybe Brenda has a lot more to her than I ever gave her credit for. I think—" and the thought was such a new one

she was astonished to hear herself putting it into words—
"I think maybe, when I got to know her better, I might like
her. I might really like her very much."

"Oh, she's a nice kid," Paul said easily. "I've been saying
that all along." He gave Lynn a worried glance. "What do
you think I ought to do? Call her mother?"

"Oh, for goodness' sake!" Lynn exclaimed. "That's the
last thing you should do. That would make an issue of the
whole thing."

"Well, do *you* want to call Brenda—"

"No," Lynn answered decidedly, "that would be even
worse. The only thing for you to do is to get back in your car
and drive over and pick her up again. You'll still have time
to make it by nine o'clock, but don't wait here until she's
changed her clothes and taken off her make-up."

"But what if she won't go?"

"She'll go," Lynn assured him. "You *make* her go, if you
have to pick her up and carry her out to the car. Tell her
she's nice to be so noble, but not to be silly about it. She's
started this debutante thing, and she's got to go ahead and
finish it." She smiled. "Only say it in a nicer way. You'll
know how to do it."

"But—" Paul was staring at her. "But what about you?
You want to go to this thing yourself. I know you do. And
I want to take you. Brenda's made her choice, so why don't
we just let her stick by it?"

"Because Brenda has had so little," Lynn said quietly, realizing it fully for the first time, "and we have so
much."

And now, because she did not have to let him go, she
found she could do it without any pain. She was Paul's girl.

Paul's girl! It was a singing inside her, a quiet shining joy that could not be dulled. Paul would always help people and stick up for people and be nice to people, because that was the kind of person Paul was. But it had nothing to do with her being Paul's girl.

They walked out to the car together. The night was dark, and the sky was heavy with stars. There was a brisk wind blowing up from the river. It was not a warm wind, winter was too recently over for that, but there was a freshness to it and a crispness and a smell of spring.

They paused a moment by the car. Paul reached out in the darkness with his good hand and found hers.

"Oh," he said casually, "I almost forgot I have something of yours."

"Of mine?" Lynn was surprised. "What is it?"

And then she felt the ring in her hand, round and hard and smooth, still warm from Paul's finger.

"That is yours," he said gruffly, "isn't it? I think maybe you lost it some place."

"Yes," Lynn answered softly, "it's mine. It's good to have it back. I—I'll take better care of it this time."

Paul got into the car.

"I'll see you tomorrow then," he said. He hesitated, as though there were more he wanted to say, and then he gave her hand a squeeze and released it. There was time ahead for saying things.

"Yes," Lynn agreed, "tomorrow."

She did not watch the car drive away. She turned instead, and went into the house.